Walter Brown

Tales, Poetry, and Fairy Tales

Third Edition

Walter Brown

Tales, Poetry, and Fairy Tales
Third Edition

ISBN/EAN: 9783337072735

Printed in Europe, USA, Canada, Australia, Japan

Cover: Foto ©Andreas Hilbeck / pixelio.de

More available books at **www.hansebooks.com**

TALES, POETRY,

AND

FAIRY TALES,

BY

WALTER BROWN.

ILLUSTRATED WITH NINETY WOODCUTS,
MANY OF WHICH ARE PRINTED FROM ORIGINAL BLOCKS BY THE FAMOUS
THOMAS BEWICK.

THIRD EDITION.

London:
220, GREAT PORTLAND STREET, W.

MDCCCLXXXIV.

Contents.

TIBBY WILTON AND THE GYPSIES.

CHAPTER I.

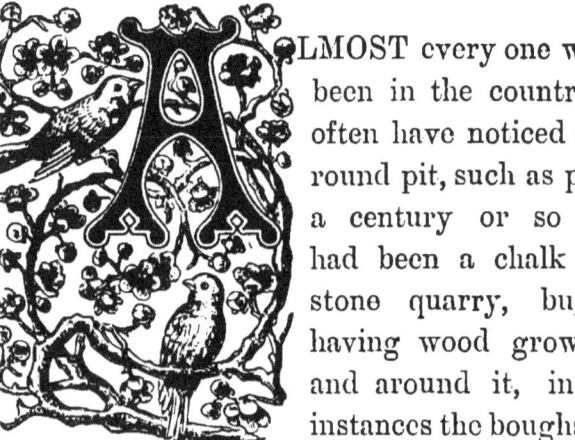 LMOST every one who has been in the country must often have noticed a large round pit, such as perhaps a century or so before had been a chalk pit or stone quarry, but now having wood growing in and around it, in some instances the boughs hanging as it were quite over at the top, and you

A

would scarcely think that they could hold on and grow there as they do. Some of the pits are a long distance across, and generally are approached by a narrow roadway, the ruts of which are covered with grass.

It was in one of these pits that three men and two women sat beside a fire which was blazing at the further end. A horse and·a large donkey were eating the grass which grew around them. A covered cart and van were standing, and a low tent with the covering nearly black with smoke, was fastened to the ground with long stakes.

A large long dog lay curled up near the fire, and every now and then he lifted up his head as if in the act of listening.

On the fire hung a large round pot; the way this was suspended was by a short chain fastened to two stakes, which were stuck in the ground.

It had just got dark, and the blaze of the fire gave a very singular effect to the different parts of the pit as it blazed up more or less.

Neither of the three men or two women spoke, for they appeared to be occupied with their own thoughts.

Presently the dog sprang upon his two fore-feet, and listened very eagerly ; in another instant he lapped his ears, as indicative of it being some-one he knew ; and in a minute or so a girl of about twelve years old could be seen coming along the pit.

She came straight up to the fire, and shot a number of large turnips upon the ground from an apron she wore.

CHAPTER II.

HE two women, without speaking, each took one of the turnips the girl had thrown down, and began peeling it, after which they threw it into the pot on the fire.

"Rather a lean scether, to-night," remarked one of the men, with his eyes fixed at the contents of the pot.

"Old Turk's out," said one of the other men; "he has been away a good hour; but suppose he has not had good luck to-night yet; at any rate, he knows it won't do for him to come back with his mouth shut;" and at that moment Old Turk, the dog alluded to, came up with a fine hare in his mouth.

One of the gypsy men (for they were gypsies)

took from his pocket a long clasp-knife, and in a few minutes had skinned the hare Turk had brought, and it was thrown into the pot.

"There is room for more than that," said one of the women, whereupon one of the men waved his hand to the two dogs, and said, "off you go," and away they went.

Not quite half-an-hour had passed when one of the dogs returned with a large fowl in his mouth; it was quite dead; he had most likely killed it to stop its making a noise, for it is wonderful to what dogs can be trained.

"That's a trifle better," said one of the gypsy-men, as he took the fowl from the dog. "Off you go, again;" and the dog readily obeyed.

The gypsy then went to another part of the pit, and soon returned with a very large lump of stiff clay; this he worked about in his hands until he had made the whole lump soft; he then cut off the head and legs, and rolled the fowl carefully up in the clay, and placed it in the middle of the fire; in time the clay became red hot; it was then in the course of an hour taken out, and put on one side to cool somewhat. The

A 3

clay was then carefully broken, and the fowl
taken out as white and beautiful as can possibly
be imagined, for the feathers and skin cling tight
to the clay.   The flavour of a fowl cooked in this
way is much superior to the usual way of
cooking.

This mode is usually adopted by gypsies when
opportunity offers.

Besides, there are several reasons, one of which
is that in the event of search being made for a
lost fowl before they had eaten it, very few would
look for it in the middle of a blazing fire.

Thomas Bewick.

CHAPTER III.

ALLY will be sure to find a child, said one of the men, in a serious mood; "or its no use us going yonder, next week. We must have one that can dance, there's no mistake about that; for that's a fair we have always done well at, and no mistake."

Whilst he was speaking another woman joined them; she had a basket on her arm, with some tape, thread, thimbles, and such things, all mixed together, as if selling them had not been the object for which she had been carrying them about.

"Out with it, Sally," said the others; "don't say, no, this time, or we are as good as done up." And they all looked at her and were silent, to hear her speak.

"Don't let your peckers fall too low," said the woman (gypsies do not use the most refined language), "for I have seen the bird you want, and I don't think knabbing it will be a very hard job." "What's its age?" inquired all of them at once. "About eight." "That will do right."

"What's the colour of her wool?" This was meant for "what colour is her hair?" "White."

"She's the bird for our net, and she shall soon be in it." Jerry and Turk each came in with a rabbit in their mouths, which were soon in the seething pot with the other things.

Old Sally then gave them a minute description of what a long and winding road it was to the house in which this beautiful and fair little girl lived, and that she appeared to be the only child, and how fond and careful her parents appeared to be of her, and that stealing her from the house would be out of the question, for her father appeared to be a gentleman farmer, and that there were a good many men employed about the place.

"It don't matter to us," said the gypsy men, "if she suits our book we will soon net her some way

or other." "I shall go and try to have a peep at her in the morning," said one.

And so he did, for he went to the house pretending to sell a few fancy baskets; one of which

the young lady thought she should like, which
her mamma immediately bought,—little thinking
for what purpose that bad and wicked man was
there,—even to see if she would suit his purpose
to steal her. The gypsies had decided upon their
plan, and only waited the opportunity to carry it
out.

One was stationed in a small wood, close to the
road from the house in which Mr. Wilton lived
(for that was his name).

" Keep yourselves ready for the start," said one
of the gypsy men, " there won't be many minutes
to spare when it does come."

The three men then went away, taking with
them a long saw and a hatchet.

About half-a-mile from Mr. Wilton's house, the
road was rather narrower, just where some tall
trees grew in a small wood. The three men crept
carefully into the wood, and two of them commenced
sawing and cutting down a large tree, whilst the
other kept watch.

They cut most of the loose boughs off the tree,
and then looked at each other as much as to say,
so far, so good.

Then there was a noise and the barking of a dog; the gypsies crouched down. They could just see the road. Presently a horse and cart came along,

a man was leading the horse; standing in the cart was a dog, barking at a boy teazing it with a stick.

CHAPTER IV.

NE of the gypsy men on the next day crept again into the wood and placed himself in such a position that he could see Mr. Wilton's house, and a large part of the road leading to it.

He watched all that day, and on the next another gypsy went to the same place and did the very same thing. And this went on for three days.

On the fourth day about three o'clock in the afternoon, Mr. Wilton, his wife and little daughter, got into the dog cart that had been taken to the front door, and along the road they came, appearing in very high spirits. Just as they were passing where the gypsy man lay concealed, Mr. Wilton's face was turned to his daughter, who had evidently been saying something that amused him very much.

"It's all very well, Tibby," said her father. "You always manage to get the right side of me."

"Of course I do, darling," said Tibby, "because I am your daughter."

And then they all laughed so loud.

The reason Mr. Wilton called his daughter "Tibby," was, not that it was her name, but because she was born near the banks of the *Tiber*, a beautiful River in Italy. For Mr. and Mrs. Wilton had travelled about a great deal.

On they went, little thinking that it was one of the happiest moments of their lives, and that they would soon be as sad as they were then happy.

It is a great and wise dispensation of Divine providence that human nature is ignorant of the future, or there would probably be a greater limit to its happiness.

And what small causes would avoid great events. The soldier upon the battle field by slightly lowering his head would thereby avoid the deadly bullet passing through his brain, to lay him lifeless amongst many of his comrades at his feet.

The sound of the wheels of Mr. Wilton's dogcart had not ceased to echo through the wood; when the gypsy with the stealth of a tiger, made

B

towards the pit, where the others were anxiously waiting.   ·

He had to be very cautious in getting from the corner of the wood; for a boy had been at a pond with a rod and line, trying to catch fish every day for the three days they had been watching.

Just as the gypsy was crawling stealthily through the bushes to get past the boy, a gentleman came up to the boy and spoke to him.

"Have you had a bite yet?" said the gentleman.

"No, sir," the boy replied.   ˎ

"But I have had a splended nibble."

The gypsy had scarcely recited what he had just seen, when the others all said "she is as safe almost as if we had got her. Before nine this very night she will be in our hands."

"WAITING FOR TIBBY."

They then began to collect the things together; greased the wheels of the cart and van, and made every preparation for a hasty start.

When it was beginning to get dark, the three men went together to the wood, and after listening some time to make certain that no one was about; they began to move the tree they had cut down towards the narrow part of the road, and in about an hour had laid it right across the road.

One of the men then with the greatest caution went back to the pit to get all in readiness.

It was now very dark and commenced raining fast; the wind was getting high, and the trees made a rustling noise by being blown about.

Every now and then there was a slight noise amongst the leaves in the wood as if a hare or rabbit was passing over them.

Presently a rabbit cried at a distance.

"*Hear that?*" whispered one gypsy to the other.

"*Quiet*, its only a rabbit got into a trap!"

Then all was still again except the wind, and that got higher every hour.

A short time, and the noise of wheels were heard at a distance. The two gypsies held their breath and listened.

"Here they come," whispered one.

"That's them, safe enough," said the other. And they both crawled a little nearer to the road.

In a few minutes voices could be heard, and then Tibby's merry laugh was quite distinct.

The wind and rain were full in their face. Mrs. Wilton was holding an umbrella over herself and husband, and Tibby was doing her best to keep hers up. The horse was going at a very fast rate, for it was a noble animal.

The two gypsies were ready to spring!

The horse evidently did not see the tree which lay across its path, at any rate not in time, for he fell with a *tremendous crash!* The shafts

C

were shivered to splinters; Mr. Wilton fell straight over the horse's head, Mrs. Wilton also fell a long way forward—Tibby fell nearer the wheels.

So sudden and violent was the fall, that all three were rendered insensible for a few minutes.

It was the work of a moment for one of the gypsies to spring out and seize Tibby, and dash into the wood with her. They then made for the pit as fast as possible, put her in the covered cart and got away as fast as they could go, and before midnight were many miles away.

As soon as Mr. Wilton came to, he crawled to the horse, which was struggling violently as it lay upon the ground. He saw his wife lying.

BUT TIBBY, OH, TIBBY! she must be under the horse!

Presently, with a little assistance from Mr. Wilton—who hastily freed the horse by cutting away the harness, the poor animal with great difficulty managed to get upon his feet, but Tibby was not to be seen. He searched amongst the ruins of the dog-cart, she was not there.

HE CALLED ALOUD FOR TIBBY, but no answer.

At last some of the men at his house heard him and came to his assistance. They got lights and searched about whilst Mrs. Wilton was being carried up to their house, but Tibby was not to be found—in fact they searched the whole night in the rain and wind, and scarcely could believe it true.

CHAPTER V.

AYLIGHT was just breaking, and the eastern sky was tinged with those long and bright red streaks which in this country indicate wet or wind, when the gypsies turned from the main road into a lane, not only because the horse and donkey required some rest, but also that they were anxious to have a view of the beautiful little Tibby whom they had stolen.

The child was naturally much frightened at the faces by which she was surrounded, and would have been glad to cry, only that her fears were too great.

"Don't cry, young 'un," said one of the gypsy women, "and we won't cut off yer head."

This was not the sort of language poor Tibby had been in the habit of hearing, and consequently was frightened accordingly.

The seething pot was got out from the cart and a fire lit, and as soon as the meat was eaten off each bone, the bone was thrown to the dogs, Jerry and Turk.

"Now then, you pests of human nature," said a voice from over the hedge, "I won't have you camping about on my farm, so off you go, and be quick about it."

This remark was from the mouth of a good old farmer, who would give milk from his dairy to any one who was not rich enough to pay for it, so that they were honest, and tried to get a living by work, "but as to a set of wandering scoundrels," said he, "they may not rob you whilst they are camping about your premises, but they take the first opportunity of doing so after they are supposed to be gone further away."

"I'll give you an hour," said the farmer, "and

if you are not off by that time, it will be the worse
for you!"

The gypsies then made their way off, and continued along the main road, feeling very much
afraid that they might be pursued, and in three
days were over a hundred miles away.

CHAPTER VI.

N the fourth day, about three o'clock in the afternoon, the cart and van came to what appeared a very large town, and after a while turned up a narrow place, which led to a large field, or rather waste piece of land.

Here a very singular scene presented itself.

A large number of gypsies, carts, vans, booths, and, in fact, all kinds of out-of-the-way things necessary for a fair were there.

Every one appeared to be so busy that they had not time to notice anything but what they were doing themselves.

In front of some of the vans they were erecting stages.

Others were fixing large round affairs, upon which were wooden horses, which are caused to go by machinery, each horse having its grand name on it in gold letters.

Some were putting up large swings; others

fixing gymnastics, and numerous other kinds of things.

Tibby had grieved ever since the night she had been taken from her parents; all her thoughts were not so much about herself as the anxiety about her father and mother. Lots of times she thought what they must think had become of her, and how they would almost break their hearts to lose her.

AND SHE FANCIED SEEING THEM BURIED BOTH IN ONE GRAVE
IN THE CHURCHYARD.

Then she would think, perhaps they were both killed with that dreadful fall from the dog-cart.

And she fancied seeing them being buried, both in one grave, in the churchyard; and then she would continue sobbing again; and so she cried until no more tears came.

The gypsies who had stolen Tibby were going about the field to get a place to fix up a stage with some other gypsies. And Tibby was left in the van with another girl, the girl who shot the turnips out of her lap in the pit.

This girl the gypsies called "Daisy," because she always looked so fresh and nice.

"Don't fret any more, dear," said Daisy to Tibby, when they were left together; "don't cry any more, dear, because you look so ill, and you can't get away, now." And then Daisy went up to Tibby, smoothed her fair hair with her hand, and kissed her.

And then Tibby spoke for the first time, and asked Daisy, "which of the gypsies were her father and mother?"

"None of them are my father and mother, dear," said Daisy; "I expect they got me in the

same way as they did you. But they have had
me so long that I do not remember any one but
them."

"What is your name, dear?" said Daisy.

"Mamma and Papa always called me 'Tibby;'"
and then she burst out crying again.

"Never mind, Tibby," said Daisy; "I will take
care of you as well as I can."

"They have never beat me since I have been
with them; but dancing so much is very tiring."

Tibby seemed surprised, which Daisy noticed
and said—

"*You* will have to dance when the fair begins."

And then Daisy told her all about it; and that
the stages they were putting up was where girls
would have to dance and act, and men, too. And
that they would have to try and please the people, in order to get money.

"Let's get where we can see more about us,"
said Daisy; and they both got out and sat on the
steps of the van.

At a distance was seen approaching a boy, carrying upon his shoulders another boy, in appearance considerably older than himself, followed by

a lot of smaller boys, all hallooing at their very loudest.

The boys who followed thought it good fun; but it was not such good fun as they imagined.

It appears that when quite a child, Caleb, the boy now upon the shoulders of the other boy had met with an accident, so serious that one of his ancles was quite dislocated, consequently he could only get a very short distance at a time, and that with great pain.

The boy, upon whose shoulders Lame Caleb now is, was one day passing along very quietly beside a hedge, when he thought he heard a noise, so, peeping through, he beheld Lame Caleb, sitting crying, and talking now and then to himself.

"Look at that swallow," said Lame Caleb, "how it glides along, and twitters as if it knew nothing but happiness, and here am I can't walk without such pain; how I wish I could run like other boys," and then Lame Caleb's feelings overcame him again, and more tears ran from his blue eyes, fast down his cheeks.

This was too much for Ralph, the boy who was on the other side of the hedge, so he

made a spring over to the side where Lame
Caleb sat.

"I heard what you said about the swallow,"
said Ralph, "so I mean to behave to you as if you
were my brother; and all the spare time I have
I shall carry you where you want to go on my
shoulders."

And Ralph kept his word, for if there was anything going on, Ralph was generally to be seen
with Lame Caleb on his shoulders; and after a
time Ralph said he got so strong that he felt quite
lost unless Lame Caleb was on his back.

At the very moment they were passing where
Tibby and Daisy were, Lame Caleb turned his
head to the boys who were running by their side
and making all kinds of mocking.

"I am very thankful," said Lame Caleb; "very
thankful."

"What have you got to be thankful for?" said
the boys.

"I AM THANKFUL YOU ARE NOT LIKE ME!" said
Lame Caleb.

Every boy seemed to deeply feel the reproof of
poor Lame Caleb; and from that time there was

not a boy but considered it a privilege to show
him every service he could.

THIS IS RALPH AND LAME CALEB JUST ENTERING THE
FAIR TO SEE SOME OF THE SPORTS.

Daisy and Tibby had not been there long
before a man came up to them. Daisy seemed to
know him, for she said to him—

" How are you, One-eyed Peter ? "

" All right," said the man ; " you have grown
since I saw you last."

This man had in his hand a brass instrument,
which he was trying to polish with a piece of
wash-leather.

" Is that the trumpet you always use ? " said
Daisy.

" Yes," said Peter, " I have blow'd as much wind
into that instrument as would carry a balloon up
to the moon."   And after a little more talk, and
Peter had told them several things to try and
make them laugh, he walked off, and presently
returned with a large cocoanut and four oranges.

Daisy tried to take Tibby's attention all she
could and keep her from thinking. And in a
short time another man came up and spoke to
Daisy.

This man was very tall and very thin ; his hair
was beginning to get very grey : on his head he
had a white hat, which appeared to have been sat

upon a good many times. No one would ever believe the trousers he wore were ever made especially for him (unless the tailor had made a great mistake) for they were quite four inches too short in the legs.

He had once been very rich. When his father died he left him a very large amount of money; but instead of trying to increase it in trade, he kept spending until it was all gone, consequently he was glad to do anything for a living.

Daisy had seen him coming before he got to them, for his head was easily to be seen above other people.

"Hulloa, long William," said Daisy, (he was called long William on account of his being so tall) "I am glad you are still alive."

"Not quite dead yet," said long William, "but I am not so young as I was *thirty years ago.*"

"Il n'y a pas le moindre doute á cela," said Daisy.

And then she laughed and looked at Tibby, and said, "Long William used to teach me some French once, but I am afraid I have forgotten a great deal of it."

E

In his hand Long William had a thin piece of wood with a round knob covered with soft leather; which he was trying to bind with a piece of brass wire, which he appeared to have got for the purpose.

" Have you broken your drum stick," said Daisy, " let me hold it whilst you mend it ;" and after that was done Daisy found a needle and some strong thread and sewed several buttons on his coat.

All these little things seemed to take Tibby's attention, and she was not quite so frightened.

The next morning a woman whom they had not seen before came to the van, and after looking at Tibby a little while, said " hold up your foot my little fairy, I think I can manage you all right," she then opened a carpet bag, and after sorting over its contents, took out a pair of white satin slippers and put one on to Tibby's foot; "the very thing," said the woman, with evident satisfaction; nothing could be better.

She then opened a box she had also brought, and took from it some white muslin dresses, trimmed with gold lace and spangles, and after fitting one each upon Daisy and Tibby, and a few other things, such as a wreath of roses for their heads, she seemed pleased at her success, and told them that they would look even nicer by night than by day.

CHAPTER VII.

S soon as it began to get dark the drums began to beat, and the music commence, the lights blazed and all was excitement.

The girls upon the different stages that had been erected walked around, and rubbed their hands, and looked quite smiling.

Daisy and Tibby, who were all in readiness, were taken to the platform upon which they were to perform, and as the woman had told them, their dresses certainly did look much grander in so great a glare of light; besides the trimmings sparkled so much more.

There were a great number upon the platform

ready to begin; when the old clown came rolling
on—head over heels, and said he had killed himself, and invited all the people to come to his
funeral. The music struck up and they danced.

Tibby's dancing appeared to cause great admir-
ation, not only from those who were dancing with
her, but also from the people who were looking on.

After this had gone on some time, they all
went further back into a large place where there
were a number of seats for the people who had
paid their money.

Daisy had to sing several songs, and then had
to act a piece with a very great fat man, who
said he should have her for his wife, and she said
he should not; so the old clown lifted her up, and
carried her whilst she slapped the fat man's face,
which caused great amusement.

And a great number of pieces they seemed to
act in one night.

No one could help laughing to see One-eyed
Peter; some said he never had but one eye; but
he must have had two, for there was the place for
it, only it was not there; but when he was blowing
his trumpet, with his cheeks swelled out, no one

could tell that he had even one-eye; at any rate you could not see it.

Long William appeared to admire the dancing of Daisy and Tibby as much as if they were his own daughters, and now and then, when he was a little more pleased than usual, he would give his drum such blows that it was quite amusing.

．　　　．　　　．　　　．　　　．

These people travelled about the country and attended the fairs, and acted in about the same way as we have described; and time went on, and Tibby had been with them nearly two years.

T. Bewick.

CHAPTER VIII.

R. AND MRS. WILTON had fretted night and day, and at last came to the conclusion that they would remove from where they were living, for there appeared no chance of ever knowing what had become of Tibby. Everything that had belonged to her, such as playthings and presents that had been made to her, were all carefully packed, and placed where they could not be seen—for they were only painful reminiscences of the past.

The horses upon which she had bestowed her approbation were even sold, as also everything constituting a nice home—all was parted with.

There was only one thing that was a favourite —yes, and a great favourite with Tibby—that Mr. Wilton said *must* still be kept, and that was a

large dog, who would have fought till death to
have protected his young mistress.

Yes! had Prince been there when the horse
fell over the tree placed across the road—no
gypsies would ever have got possession of Tibby,
for he was a desperate dog to a foe.

So, when all was sold, Mr. and Mrs. Wilton
went to reside in another part of the country.

No man knew better than Mr. Wilton that a
life of inactivity is the most oppressive under
which any one can exist, so he purchased more
land than he had so lately disposed of, and planted
orchards of the very choicest graftings.   He also
built good cottages for those whom he employed,
for he found that many of his men were quite tired
in the morning when they came to their work, on
account of having miles to walk, through living
so far away.

It was now nearly two years since Tibby had
been stolen, and, of course, Mr. Wilton could
not form the least idea whether she was alive or
dead; for, from the time the horse fell, nothing
further was known, no more than if the earth had
opened and swallowed her up, or a cloud from

above had come down and borne her away; at
any rate, as far as her parents knew.

It was a nice bright afternoon that Mr. and
Mrs. Wilton were sitting in their new home;
every now and then Mr. Wilton would raise his
eyes, and appear to be noticing the beautiful landscape.

"I think it would do you good to go and have
a drive," said Mrs. Wilton, who noticed daily her
husband's increased dejection.

"So I will," said Mr. Wilton; "I have some
things to order from the town;" and in a short
time he had started.

It was about seven miles to the town to which
Mr. Wilton went, so he drove to the White Swan,
for he had some slight acquaintance with the
gentleman who kept that hotel.

Mr. Houghton, who was the proprietor of that
establishment, and who knew of Mr. Wilton's
grief for his daughter, sympathized with him very
much; so after Mr. Wilton had completed his
business in the town, Mr. Houghton prevailed
upon him to stay and take some tea.

Mr. Houghton then desired his daughters to
play and sing some pretty songs.

"What do you say to a stroll," said Mr. Houghton, "before you start. I hear there is a *fair* up in a field, not half-a-mile away; suppose we go and see what's going on;" so they both started.

When they arrived at the fair they found all kinds of diversions going on, and were considerably amused with what they saw.

And they began to think of making their way towards the White Swan.

Presently they heard a tremendous noise, more like large guns going off than anything else they could think of.

"What a tremendous noise," said Mr. Wilton; "what can that be?" and they both listened, and soon heard it again.

"It *must* be a drum," said Mr. Houghton; "but I never heard one beat in that style; let us walk up to that part of the fair;" and they did so.

The reason of this was that Daisy and Tibby were dancing to such perfection that Long William was so delighted to see them, that he was slashing at his drum beyond all bounds, and that was the cause of it.

There were more people round this stage than any other in the fair, and it took the two gentlemen some time to get sufficiently near to see.

"What a lovely girl that fair one is," said Mr. Houghton; "she looks too good for that sort of work;" and at last they managed to get nearly close up, and the people were clapping their hands with great delight as the dance had finished.

Then there was a loud scream from Tibby, who rushed to the front of the stage and cried out—

"OH! MY DARLING PAPA!"

In an instant Mr. Wilton had bounded upon the platform, and Tibby and him were clasped in each others arms.

   .   .   .   .   .

That night the three gypsy men who stole Tibby were in gaol.

   .   .   .   .   .

We shall now leave our young readers just to imagine Mr. Wilton and Tibby going home together that evening, and Mrs. Wilton's feelings on their arrival.

DICK WHITTINGTON AND THE KING.

"HARK, WHAT ARE THOSE BELLS SAYING."

When Dick Whittington became a man,
And Lord Mayor of London fine,
He thought one day he would invite
The King with him to dine.

He made a fire of scented wood,
  Which from foreign countries came,
The King admired its pleasant scent,
  Likewise its brilliant flame.

Said Whittington a bond I hold
  For twenty thousand pounds,
For which I paid you all in gold,
  As bright as could be found.

But money seems so scarce with you,
  And plenty still I've got,
A good King you have been to me—
  Who dare say you have not ?

A brighter flame you soon shall see,
  My great liege Lord and King,
The bond right in the fire straighway,
  He manfully did fling.

The King in rapture saw the flame
  Destroy this heavy bond,
And vow'd a nobler man than Dick,
  Was no where to be found.

All thanks, all thanks to Whittington,
  The King cried out aloud,
Of a subject such as noble Dick,
  The best King might be proud.

F

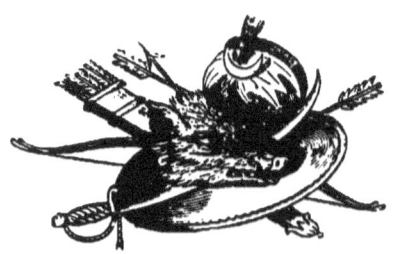

OGRE THE SLASHER.

(DEDICATED TO FRANK LEONARD.)

NCE upon a time, in a Castle standing on a high hill, mostly surrounded by wood, lived a giant of immense height ; so tall was he that each of his legs measured nearly five feet in length, and by his general appearance you would think he could eat almost any amount of food without being satisfied.

He never left his castle in the day, but at night he would sally forth and make sad havoc amongst the cattle of the surrounding farmers and villagers. He was held in such dread that almost everyone was afraid to be out after dark.

Some years before, a number of men tried to take him, but he drew a long sword, and so cut and slashed before and behind, that he killed nearly all of them; from that time he was called "OGRE the SLASHER," and was more feared than before.

At night, as soon as it was very dark, he would come down from his Castle and scour the surrounding fields and take sheep or oxen; he has been seen to go up to his castle with a sheep under each arm. He would run a bullock down in a few minutes, when he would put out his full strength and break its neck, and would generally manage to get it to his castle without cutting it in half; and he became so dreaded by all around, that he spread more terror than if a lion had taken his abode round about. At length, things began to get to such a state that the people found that they must leave that part, or something must be done to capture "Ogre." They met a great many times to talk it over, and could not think of any plan to attack him, unless it was when he came out at night; but then, knowing how fierce he was, the wives and daughters of the farmers and villagers shed so many tears, that it prevented them from attempting that mode of procedure.

Time went on, and every one that had an ox or a sheep soon lost it. At last things became so desperate that it was agreed to attack him in his castle. So a day was arranged for all the men to meet and go armed with bludgeons, and burst the immense castle door open, and take him dead or alive, as best they could.

It was really painful to see the little children kissing their fathers before they started, every child thinking that if anyone was killed it would sure to be his father, and wives thinking the same of their husbands.

At length the morning came when the attack was to be made, and trumpets were blown, and the men all started for the castle. Some rode on horses, some walked. After battering at the door for some time, presently an immense stone was thrown from the inside of the castle yard, which would have killed several men if it had fallen on them ; unfortunately it struck a horse and killed it.

This convinced the men they must not get too near, and for a time they did not know what to do.

At last some of them thought it would be better

to send and get a large quantity of gunpowder, and blow the gates away; so two were despatched on horses to get it, and it was placed against the castle gates, and a torch lit, and all the men immediately got a distance off.

Presently the explosion took place, shivering the gates all to splinters, and making a report which was heard many miles round.

In dashed all the men together, when in the the courtyard they saw Ogre with his slashing sword as if he would soon kill all of them, and everyone seemed afraid; at last a gentleman amongst them and who was rich, called out with a loud voice; A HUNDRED POUNDS FOR THE MAN WHO STRIKES THE FIRST BLOW AT HIM. This frightened Ogre as much as it inspired the others, and all made a desperate rush towards him; but Ogre saw at a glance that they were desperate, and away he went and in about six strides was through a long passage and making for the top tower of the Castle, where he tore great stones from the walls and hurled them down; but he was followed so closely that he dashed into another tower and fastened himself in. On went

the men after him, and commenced with their
cudgels battering at the door, and in about a
quarter of an hour they were glad to find the door
began to crack; they then all together put their
shoulders to the door, and at the word put out
their full strength and in went the door with a
crash, all of them falling headlong into the room
where Ogre was.

Whilst they were on the ground, Ogre with a
desperate leap bounded over them, and made for
another tower, which had no connection with that
part of the Castle. It was an immense jump,
but it was now the only chance left, and if he did
not accomplish it his fall would be over a hundred
feet to the courtyard below. So he was on the
parapet in an instant, and a most desperate spring
he made, but the fates were against him this
time, for he sprang with such force that one
of the large stones gave way beneath his feet,
and headlong he fell into the deep courtyard
below.

When the men had hurried again down the
large stone stairs, it took them some time to find
the place where Ogre had fallen; at last they

found him, laying upon his back quite dead, a great number of his bones appearing to be broken. When all the men had assembled around him they gave an immense shout of "Hurrah" and "death to Ogre the Slasher!" They then took his body and tied it with cords across two of the horses and formed a procession towards the nearest village, where all the wives and children were awaiting their return.

BILL JOHNSON.

Bill Johnson was a naughty boy ;
　When he was young his father died;
He danced about the house that day,
　His mother she sat down and cried.

When he was started off to school,
　Bill always went another way ;
He stammered so tremendously,
　You scarce could tell what he did say.

In summer time the fields he'd roam,
　And find birds' nests with half a look ;
He would not work, he could not read,
　He hated the very name of · *book*.

Bill never liked to tell the truth,
　But falsehood was his great delight ;
Whenever little boys he met,
　He always urged them on to fight.

T. Bewick.

His grandfather was almost blind,
    And scarce could see his way along;
When he asked Bill the way to go,
    He always led him in the pond.

One day his mother dressed him well,
    And made him look so smart and prim;
But when they got to the church door,
    She could not make him to go in.

His mother said one day to him,
    O Billy, you do very wrong;
Unless you mend your evil ways,
    The day will come when you'll be hung.

A little boy went to a pond,
    With rod and line to catch some fish;
He was a good brave little boy,
    And obeyed his parents slightest wish.

Bill Johnson saw that little boy,
    And to himself said " this is fine,
I'll go and push him in that pond,
    And bolt off with his rod and line."

The little fellow fought with Bill,
  And clung to him with all his might;
Bill tried in vain to throw him off,
  But the little fellow clung too tight.

At last they both fell in that pond,
  For all around was rising ground,
A dog dragged out the little boy,
  BILL JOHNSON—he was DROWN'D.

THE SOUTHEYS AND THE LIONS.

"Do you think in another year," said Mr. Southey's three little sons and two daughters, "that you will be able to get sufficient for us to go?"

"As far as I can judge at present," replied the father, "I think there is not the least chance of it; for I am realizing less money every year, and am almost afraid to think how I shall be able to provide for you, and I quite tremble to think of it."

This conversation was the result of a long cherished hope that the day would come when Mr. Southey with his wife, three fine little fellows, and two girls, would be able to go abroad to where they had heard land was to be purchased very cheap, and where they could cultivate it, and soon have a nice farm of their own; for they all were very anxious to get away from the sort of life they lived in London.

At Mr. Southey's reply, that there appeared not the slightest hope of all their wishes, they were very much cast down.

"Suppose you sell everything you have," replied some of them, "and all the furniture, I should think that would be enough to pay the expenses of getting there."

"Perhaps it would nearly do that," said Mr. Southey, " but to arrive in a strange land without money or home, would be very deplorable indeed." And they all seemed very sad.

Since this last remark no one had spoken, and each seemed to be occupied with their own unwelcome thoughts.

They were somewhat startled by a knock at the door by the letter carrier, bringing a letter.

" I do not much like the look of this," said, Mr. Southey, as one of his little sons gave the letter into his hands, " It looks like some lawyer's letter," and he appeared very reluctant to open it, fearing something was wrong ; but at last he did open it, and after reading it twice, he read it aloud, and who was the most astonished it was impossible to judge.

This was the contents :

" To Mr. Southey,

" Sir,—I herewith beg to inform you that

Mrs. Emily Southey, who died three weeks since, and who was a distant relation of your father, has in her *will* left to you the sum of one thousand five hundred pounds, which money you can receive on applying at my office."

It was now impossible to tell which of them looked the most pleased and surprised.

On that very day Mr. Southey went to Lincoln's Inn to the lawyer's office, and received a cheque for that large amount of money.

Mr. Southey then went to the Bank of England and gave the cheque to one of the numerous clerks who pay money out.

The clerk looked at the cheque carefully, and then said to Mr. Southey, " How will you take this, sir ? "

" In money," said Mr. Southey.

" Yes," answered the clerk, " but what kind of money ?"

" Oh, all in sovereigns," said Mr. Southey.

The clerk immediately took some large weights and put into some scales which were on the counter, and began shovelling golden sovereigns into the scale with a small shovel. When he had weighed five hundred he shot them upon the counter before Mr. Southey and said, "There will be two more lots like that."

"Oh!" said Mr. Southey, "My pockets will not hold so much money.

"Of course they will not," said the clerk smiling, "You had better take most of it in bank notes."

So he had it in bank notes and fifty sovereigns, and even then the sovereigns were too heavy for one pocket.

When Mr. Southey got home you may imagine what they all thought at the sight of so much money.

In less than a month after this, Mr. Southey, his wife, three sons and two daughters were on board the vessel, which was to take them to the distant land.

And although having so much money that they were able to provide themselves with comforts, still before they got there, they were now and then almost inclined to wish they had not started; for sometimes the wind would blow what the sailors called *great guns*, and the sea run almost

mountains high; sometimes the vessel would be
held high up on the top of a wave and immediately after almost buried below, but at last they
arrived safe at port.

Whilst it was being decided where the land lay
which was to be their future home, they were busy
buying such things as would be required for use
and comfort. And they soon started in a long
covered van drawn by ten oxen; and after considerable difficulties mixed with excitement and

pleasure, at last arrived safe at the long desired haven.

The first thought was to build a temporary house, although the weather was warm; some people who had gone out in a similar way and had already settled, on hearing of the arrival of their new neighbours, came immediately and rendered every assistance, supplied them with almost everything they required, and helped them to build the house.

It is the usual custom to help each other in this way. Although none of the farmers like any one to come and settle nearer than five miles to them, for they say they are too crowded and cannot get sufficient air.

At any rate by perseverance things soon began to assume a more pleasant aspect, and the cows gave splended milk, the fowls and other poultry laid plenty of eggs. The seeds which they had brought from England soon sprang up, and Mr. Southey and his family rejoiced in this change of life.

The thing that astonished them most was the rapidity with which everything grew.

There was a great quantity of game besides wild turkeys, geese, ducks, widgeon, teal, &c., which occasionally might be seen in flocks of hundreds at a time.

There was also an abundance of deer of different kinds; now and then a herd of buffalo might be seen crossing from one part to another.

Mr. Southey and the two eldest boys provided a great quantity of game and other things with their double-barrel guns; and altogether it was

impossible for anyone to enjoy greater abundance
of good things than they did.

They would often receive and return visits to
their neighbours, none of which lived nearer than
five or six miles, as we have stated, because they
did not like to be crowded.   But then it did not
take long to ride six or seven miles, as they might
drive as fast as they pleased without any fear of
running over anyone.

On one dark night the dogs barked and behaved

in an unusual manner, and Mr. Southey and his
sons went out to try and ascertain the reason;
they found the oxen in one corner of their yard,
huddled close together, and trembling violently,
and were searching further when they heard a

most tremendous roar, which convinced them that it could be nothing but a lion, and they could see the glare of eyes further on in the dark.

What was to be done; they did not want to lose the oxen, yet to proceed one step further or even to stay another moment where they were might be death, so they prudently made again for the house, the dogs sticking up their backs and barking furiously.

Soon after they heard an immense noise as if a great weight was falling upon the ground, and then a faint groaning, and soon all was still.

It looked at that moment as if Mr. Southey and his sons would have gone out again and risked their lives, only they were restrained by the entreaties of Mrs. Southey and her daughters, who whilst she clung to her husband, the girls did the same to their brothers, and at last prevailed.

When the morning light began to peep it was soon clear what had taken place. There lay a fine bullock dead, with the flesh eaten along one side of the neck and part of the shoulder; the ground all round being torn about in the fatal scuffle.

The guns were got out and loaded with bullets, and Mr. Southey and his three sons started on the lions sphor, or track, and they followed until he had entered a forest about four miles off ; it was then necessary to exercise the greatest caution in their mode of proceedure, so they crept along under trees and over bushes several miles, still feeling quite confident of the track; for every now and then they could get quite a clear impression of his feet upon the softer ground.

It was necessary to exercise the greatest care as they might at any moment come upon him and he would have sprung upon and torn them down in a moment.

They were just out of a thicket that it was with difficulty they had got through, when one of them looking forward beheld something ahead under some tall trees, it was some time before they could make out what it was; but it evidently was something very large, and every now and then a part of it moved, and was quiet for a few minutes; then the same move was made again, and they laid and watched for a good while.

At length they ventured to creep a little nearer, and could soon clearly discover two immense lions. The lion was laying full length, and every few minutes threw up his head in order to drive off the flies that worried him about the nose, he also often switched his tail. The lioness lay with her chin upon her fore-feet, and appeared to listen to the least noise.

Mr. Southey and his sons looked at each other as much as to say, "this is not a pleasant place to be in, a large wood with two fierce lions close before them;" it only wanted one of them to tread upon a dry stick or make the least noise, and both lions would have been upon them in a moment. So they stood a short time, and then Mr. Southey motioned to his sons how they had better act, as even a wisper would have been dangerous.

It was that they were to get a little closer and

then two fire at the head of the lion, and two at the lioness.

They crawled on very cautiously within a reasonable distance, but were afraid of venturing nearer as the lioness seemed restless. At last they all put their guns to their shoulders, and fired together.

The lion appeared to be hard hit, but the lioness sprang into the air, and appeared at a loss to know from whence they had been interfered with; she dashed about as if ready for revenge, and then sprung to a thicket just opposite to where Mr. Southey and his sons were. They had scarcely time to take breath when she returned closely followed by two cubs. She appeared furious; catching sight of her assailants she dashed towards them with eyes flashing, and roaring tremendously.

Mr. Southey and his sons had but an instant each to spring up a tree before she was as it were upon them.

She dashed about looking up at first one and then the other, lashing her sides with her tail. She flew at one of the guns that lay upon the ground—for they had no time to get them up the trees. After a time she went to the lion, who was not yet dead, as much as to say, "Come and help," but blood was flowing from his head.

The cubs ran were their mother went as fast as they could.

Presently she dashed off again into the thicket, when one of Mr. Southey's sons sprang to the ground, seized his gun, and dragged it up the tree after him; but he was only just in time, for she was after him in an instant, and seemed not inclined to give them another chance.

But being up a tree, when a fierce lion is under it, with a gun loaded with bullet, makes another affair of it, for he took good steady aim (but not very steady, for he trembled a good deal), at any

rate he took aim, and with the barrel that had not
been discharged, sent the bullet through her
shoulder, which appeared to enrage her more than
ever.

She still lashed her sides with her tail, and
dashed about furiously; but the gun was soon
reloaded, and a couple more bullets laid her dead
upon the ground.

The cubs then made into the thicket, and after
satisfying themselves the lioness was quite dead,
Mr. Southey and his sons got down and took their
guns—for they were very doubtful about the lion—
they thought he might be only wounded, but they
soon calculated he was quite dead.

They then set to and skinned the lion and
lioness, and bore their skins off in great triumph
towards home.

On the next day they got some help and went
in search of the two cubs, and managed to secure
without killing them.

Those were the last two lions that were seen in
those parts. The two cubs were sent to England.

As to Mr. Southey and his sons, the news
spread as fast as a forest on fire; and all the

farmers for at least fifty miles, came to thank
them for their bravery, and to look at the skins

of the two monsters that had committed such
destruction and terror in every part where they
had taken up their quarters.

THE OLD WOMAN WHO WENT UP TO THE MOON.

THERE was an Old Woman one fine afternoon,
She vow'd she would take a trip up to the moon;
When the neighbours had heard this very strange
    news,
Some came out in their stockings, some in their
    shoes.

Some looked very grave, some very glad,
Others said surely she must be quite mad;
But certain it was, that agreed they all were,
She never could mount up so high in the air.

At length the Old Woman appeared in full trim,
Looking so pleasant, so smart, and so prim;
Not a tear in her eye, only smiles could be seen,
She looked quite as happy, and grand as a Queen.

In her hand she carried a very long broom,
And bid all her neighbours a fine afternoon;
Then quickly mounting high into the air,
Laughing to see how the people did stare.

She was soon lost in view to her neighbours below,
Who wondered to see at what speed she did go,
Never resting at all in her very long flight,
So anxious was she to get there before night.

The sun it went down, and was soon lost to view,
And when darkness set in, she scarce knew what
    to do;
But quickly her fears began to decline,
When she saw in its splendour, the moon brightly
    shine.

No one did she meet to say just " Good Day,"
Nor did she require to be asking her way;
But just about midnight as near as could be,
She arrived there quite safe,—as safe as could be.

So astonished was she at the very strange scene,
She had seen nothing like it where'er she had been;
Not a house, not a field, not a flower or a tree,
But all looked as funny and strange as could be.

How she was to descend put her in a sad fright,
She had nothing to eat, and a good appetite;
Till a rainbow appeared, and she slid quickly down,
And found herself safely again on the ground.

ROGER HARDWOOD.
DEDICATED TO FLORENCE.
A Fairy Tale.

DEATH having taken her husband (who had been a small farmer), his widow was sold out of house and home, and was on her way to some other part of the country, accompanied by her little son Roger. Their way lay through a large wood, and Roger, seeing so many things to interest him, allowed his mother to get considerably in advance of him, as she was anxious to get away from the scene of her late loss and troubles.

Little Roger was just thinking he must push on
and overtake his mother, when he saw a poor
crippled bird, struggling to flutter up to a bough
of a tree in order to get out of the way of a stoat
which was pursuing it, in order to devour it.
Having a stick in his hand, he rushed at the stoat
and drove it away to a distance off, and quickly

taking the bird in his hand, jumped as high as he
could, and placed it in the tree where it was
safe.　After he had done so, he felt very glad to
think he had succeeded in saving the poor bird
from being devoured, and was looking up at it,
wondering how it would get down for food, or if
it would be starved to death, when a very fine

mist began to surround it, and soon its form was increased and changed into that of a very beautiful creature somewhat resembling a lady.

So astonished was Roger, that at first he could scarcely believe his own eyes. It spoke to him in a voice which was both sweet and kind, and addressed him thus :—

" Tell me your name, little boy, for I am a fairy, and can be of great assistance to you. I was not in such danger as you supposed, but only tried the goodness of your heart, for I know that most boys are cruel."

After this surprise, he said, " My name is Roger Hardwood, and I am following my mother through this wood, but do not know where we are going, for we have been turned out of our home.

"Then I see you are not rich," said the fairy.

" I have only three farthings in my pocket," said Roger, putting his hand and touching the outside of his pocket.

He had no sooner taken his hand away, than the fairy gently struck his pocket with a hazel stick she had in her hand, and told him to hasten after his mother.

Roger ran as fast as he could, and had gone a
very long way, when he met his mother coming
back again after him, for she was very cross that he
had stayed behind. She took him by the hand,

and they went on until it began to get dusk, when
she said they must look out for a barn in
which to sleep, telling him they could not have
anything to eat as she had not any money. Upon
this, Roger told his mother of his three farthings,

and she was very glad, saying she would buy some
bread; and Roger took it out of his pocket like
a man, and gave it to her. But when she looked
at it, she saw it was three golden sovereigns, and
not three farthings, upon which she was very
much astonished. So she went into the first shop

they came to, and bought something very nice for
supper, and soon found a very comfortable place
to sleep, with a cheerful fire to sit by.

In the morning they started again, and continued many days, until Roger was taken very

sick and ill, and his mother nursed him in a room she hired.

All their money was spent but a few pence, when he got better, and being afraid of staying in a place they had not the means of paying for, they started again, his mother not having the least idea where she was going,—only that she wanted to get as far as she could from the place where her husband had died. As they journeyed along, the sun became very hot, and being wearied, they sat down under a large spreading oak tree, and Roger's mother fell asleep.

Soon he heard his name called very softly, he looked all around, and could see nothing, and thought he must have been mistaken.

He heard it again, this time very distinctly, and felt sure he could not be mistaken, and on looking up, saw the fairy in the tree above his head. He was so pleased that he did not know what to do. He told the fairy how very ill he had been; upon which the fairy pointed to a very grand house standing on a hill a short distance off, saying "you must sleep there to-night," upon which he felt very much surprised. The fairy at the same time touching his pocket with the hazel wand, departed.

Soon the sky became very black with clouds, and a tremendous thunderstorm commenced. Roger awoke his mother, and they both ran to-

wards the house and begged for shelter. The porter who opened the gate would only let them go just inside until he had been and asked his master, who came immediately himself and said he was glad to give them shelter from so dreadful a storm; he also told his servants to take care of them, and let them have a good supper and a bed, as he would not allow them to go on their journey that night.

Now, it so happened that the Baron of this mansion had a daughter, of which he was excessively fond, for she was his only child; and she lay dangerously ill, and continued to get worse day by day, which drove the good old

Baron nearly to distraction, for she was all he had in the world to care for, her mother having died when Linda (for that was the Baron's daughter's name) was very young. When Linda

heard that her father had taken a little boy and his mother to protect them from the raging storm she was very glad, and kissed her father for being so good, at the same time signifying her desire to see the little boy before he went away in the morning, which was complied with, as she never asked anything within reason but what it was granted her.

In the morning the Baron took little Roger to the room in which Linda was laying ill, and when she saw him she seemed pleased, and asked him many questions, and she was very pleased to hear him talk; after which she appeared more cheerful, for having no brother or sister, she had never spoken to any one of her own age; she had been used only to grown up people, which is not natural to children, consequently she had become

I

very dull. Upon her father noticing this he reproved himself very much, and asked Roger's mother if she would stay and help to nurse his daughter if he paid her for it; for which she was very glad. So Roger staid also, and Linda got much better every week until she was able to leave her bed, and it pleased her very much to read amusing tales to Roger out of some nice books she had.

It happened after Roger had been at the mansion a long time that the good old Baron was taken very ill and died, which grieved Roger almost as much as if it had been his own father, for Roger was sensible of all the kindness the good Baron had shown him, and had lost no opportunity to please and show all the return he could for so much kindness.

He felt sure the Baron thought a great deal of him, and in that he was quite right, which we shall see, for after the good old Baron was buried it was found he had made a will leaving all his money and lands to his daughter; and requesting that she should let Roger manage the estate, for which she was to pay him a large sum of money

every year, as he had always shown himself to be so clever and persevering. This displeased the Baron's servants very much, as they thought they would now be able to do as they pleased, but it was of all things the one which was most pleasing to Linda, as she knew her father had shown and told Roger a very great deal. So time went on, and as Roger grew bigger so he managed the estate better, and by the time he had grown to be a man he had so managed that the estate was worth double as much as when the good old Baron died; and after a time Roger was married to Linda, and very happy they both were.

Roger's mother always lived at the mansion, and had all the comforts of life; and was often heard to say "Bless the day that Roger helped the poor bird into the tree."

CLUNA CLUFF.

OLD Cluna Cluff was an Emperor bold,
  But his Empire is now passed away;
A better and braver than Old Cluna Cluff,
  Never breathed air in his day.

His subjects and he were on excellent terms,
  They were glad to do all he desired;
In his turn good Old Cluna was always inclined,
  To supply them with all they desired.

Of eating and feasting I've often heard tell,
  His subjects and he did delight;
They commenced in the morning, continued all
    day,
  And never would finish till night.

Their climate was hot, so they never forgot
To cool their parched mouths with good wine ;
It might almost be said that the wine itself made,
For grapes grew in abundance so fine.
    They had the very best cooks,
        The choicest of wine ;
    Their wives they were beautiful,
        Their horses were fine.
    One day good Old Cluna
        His subjects did call ;
    And unto them said
        " Now, list to me all :
    My wealth so alarmingly
        Great it has grown,
    That I really can not count
        The gold that I own.
    So, now, you, my good subjects,
        I wish you to know,
    I have a plan in my mind
        I should like just to show.
    Let's say this day week,
        That you all meet me here ;
    And let every man state
        What he doth require.

But keep nothing back
   Of what you require;
And I'll give you my word
   You shall have your desire."

That week past away
   As weeks always do;
Before you begin them
   You seem to be through.

So his subjects assembled
   Both the small and the great;
And there Cluna sat
   In his chair of grand state.

" Approach my brave subjects,"
   Great Cluna did say;
" And you that want something
   Just step up this way."

But no one appeared
   Inclined to proceed;
The reason of which was,
   They stood in no need.

At last a brave subject,
   Amongst them well known,

Approached in obedience
  Before Cluna's throne.
" Great Cluna," said he,
  " The cause of your wealth,
Is the fruits of not ruling
  For entirely yourself.

But you've ruled us so well,
  That our wealth it has grown
In abundance, quite equal
  Unto your own.

So nothing we want;
  But your goodness so great,
Shall in letters of gold
  Shine throughout all the state."

Then brave Old Cluna
  Did unto them say,
" You subjects so bold,
  Just hear what I say :
Since all of us have
  Such abundance of wealth,
Fill up all our goblets,
  And drink to our health."

T. Bewick.

THE LITTLE DOVE.

ANYONE having noticed the skylark rise from the ground, and as he gradually ascended into the bright beautiful atmosphere, even futher than the eye could follow him, and listening to those notes so full of beauty, and poured forth in such rapture and explosive harmony, must have experienced great delight.

The good old mill stood there with its winding stairs, and many generations of millers, ever ready to receive and deliver in full weight the grist brought by pretty village maidens, had from one to one passed away; but still the old, the dear familiar old mill was there, waving its long sails in circular motion.

The miller was singing with all that joy and hilarity indicative of his nature.

He had two children who strictly inherited that buoyancy of life so peculiar and characteristic of himself.

And if you might gauge human nature by his standard, you would naturally come to the conclusion that trouble and sorrow were quite unknown to this world.

It was one morning at breakfast—they always had breakfast early, for they experienced such strength and lightness of spirits, to which later risers are quite strangers—when little Bessie, the miller's daughter, with flushed cheeks told her father and mother that she had had such a pretty dream.

How the miller did laugh, and told her to say what she had dreamed.

So she began and said, " She dreamed that she and her little brother Frank wandered a long way into a beautiful wood, where all was so lovely and all things seemed to harmonize with each other ; and that after wandering a long time in the wood, suddenly found a little *Dove*, and that they brought it home and kept it, and that their home was much more happy than it was before."

The miller laughed heartier than ever, and said it tickled his fancy wonderfully; and then he laughed until the water ran out of his eyes and all down his cheeks.

How he did laugh.

The next morning his little daughter asked him if she might with her brother go into the wood and try and find the little dove she had dreamed of. He told her she might do so, and then he had another good laugh.

So they were soon ready and started.

It was a beautiful spring morning, and they entered the wood where

> " Every thing seemed made to please."

For the birds were singing in the trees; the bees and insects were humming around the flowers, every now and then a little rabbit would run out of the long grass from beneath their feet, bobbing his little white tail, as much as to say " mind you do not tread upon me."

Then a wild pigeon would flutter out of the

branches of a tree above their heads, fearing they
were come to take the eggs from its nest.

The little robin red-breast would sit low upon
a branch and not appear at all afraid of them.

The pretty little harmless lizards shot rapidly

about the heath-stems, as much as to say "do not tread upon my little slender tail." Then there was a cooing of the ring-dove in the branches of a high tree, and Frank looked up as much as to say "it is you we are come after," but it soon flew away.

They had now got a long way into the wood, and began to think they should have to go home without any little dove, so they sat down under a large tree, and picked some very pretty yellow primroses which grew so thick that the ground seemed quite yellow. And then they thought they would go on "just a little further" and then turn back and go home.

So they did go a little further than they intended, and were just going to turn and go back, when Bessie said, "Frankie" (his mother and Bessie often called him that, but his father called him Frank), so she said "Frankie shall we go back home, I am so sorry we cannot find the little dove."

"Why we saw it in the tree," said little Frank.

"No Frankie," said Bessie, "The one I dreamed about was on the ground."

K

. And they went on a little further.

They were just going to turn to go back, when they saw a sort of little hut, made of hurdles,

thatched with long grass; they could not see any-one, so they went a little nearer and then stood still, but no one appeared to be there.

They could see a pretty little garden as if it had been made by a child; for there were many little innocent looking wild flowers planted in it; there was also some wild honey-suckle tied to a stick with rushes, and it had nice blossoms on it; but still they could not see any one about.

So they went peeping about, and got round the other side of the hut; they made no noise, but went very softly. There they saw a little girl sitting with a quantity of fresh gathered flowers in her lap, trying to arrange them into a little, nosegay. They stood quite still, for she had not seen them.

In a few moments she raised her head, and then they could tell she saw them.

She immediately hung down her head, and did not even touch her flowers.

And for some time Bessie and Frank stood still and looked at her.

Then they went a little nearer, and by degrees got almost close to her: but still she did not speak.

At last little Bessie said, "Do you live here, little girl?"

She did not speak but shook her head, and then began crying.

Bessie took the little apron she was wearing, and wiped the large bright tears as they ran down her cheeks; and then little Frankie almost began to cry.

So, after she had left off crying, Bessie asked her where her father and mother were, but she said she had neither, but the men who took care of her were smugglers, and that they had always taken care of her; but that she heard them say that the officers were after them, and that they went away in a great hurry and said that if they could they would come back and fetch her, but she said they had been gone three days, and that she feared they could not come back again for her, and then she cried again as if her little heart would break.

Bessie did not know what to do, for she was so sorry. So she sat down beside the little girl and kissed her. And then she asked her to come home with them; but the little girl shook her head and said she had no one to take care of and love her.

Then Bessie told her how glad her father and mother would be for her to come and live with them.

So they each took hold of her hand, and began to go through the wood towards their home, and at last they got there.

Now when they had got into the house, their mother was busily engaged taking out of a large iron pot which was on the fire, a plain plum pudding; so when she heard children's footsteps, she said, without looking round, " Well, have you found the little dove ? "

" Yes, mother," was the reply, " and brought it home with us."

Just at that moment there was a tremendous loud voice at a distance, singing as it came along

> " The feathered warbling songsters
> Their notes so charming sweet did tune."

" Here comes father," said Bessie and Frank and then their father came in.

He appeared very much surprised, but also very pleased when they told him what they had done. And after a time they all sat down to the dinner.

The miller took the " Little Dove " and sat her in a chair beside him, and cut her a large piece of the pudding to begin with ; and Bessie and Frank each sat as close to her as they possibly could.

They all soon grew very fond of her, and she could soon run up and down the steps of the mill quite as fast as Bessie and Frank. And often as they all sit around the cheerful fire in the winter evenings they laugh and say how glad they are that Bessie dreamed about

THE LITTLE DOVE.

THE YOUNG LORD.

DEDICATED TO GREVILLE HOWARD.

NOT long ago, there was a great Lord, who lived in a castle in the country. He had pleasant fields, where the buttercups and cowslips grew in the summer, that it looked almost like a covering of gold. He had also large woods, where the birds sung from morning until night. He had a little son, whom the people that lived on the estate called the Young Lord.

Now it happened one day that the young lord and his nurse went out to walk in the pleasant fields and lanes, which they often did when the weather was fine, that the young lord, running after a butterfly, got a very long way from his nurse, and could not find his way back. All at once he came upon a tribe of gipsies, camping in a pit, who, as soon as they saw him, ran to him, and he was so frightened that he began to cry. They pulled him into their tent, and made him keep quite still. His nurse called as loud as she could, and, when it got dark, went and told his father and mother she had lost him.

The old lord called all his gardeners and servants, and they all went, with lanthorns, into the woods, but could not find him, for the gipsies took up their tent and the young lord and made off as fast as they could.

At last the old lord said—

CHAPTER II.

"Bring out my Milk-white Steed,"

and off he galloped to the woods. He had got a long way when, passing through a very narrow track, "where there was a high bank on each side, the boughs oftimes meeting and touching his face," when he heard a rustling in the wood, as something coming towards him.

Then he saw two eyes like balls of fire, which came straight to him. At this moment he felt so alarmed that his hair seemed almost to lift his hat from his head, but, summing up courage, he turned his bull's-eye lanthorn full upon it, and what was his delight when he found it was his " NOBLE DOG NERO."

Nero and his young master loved each other exceedingly. Although Nero was a powerful and desperate dog with an enemy, he was equally kind and gentle with his young master. Nero appeared to understand that his young master was lost, and was quite ready, and seemed better to know how to find him.

As soon as his master had given him the word, " *Find him, Nero,*" off he started, and, after some time, his master heard him barking most furiously a long distance off. After a time, Nero came back to his master, panting in a great state of uneasiness, as much as to say—"We are not doing it right. We must keep closer together."

His master could not at all understand what he

wanted, as he would go a little distance and then come back again.

At last it occurred to his master that the dog wanted to light him. So he immediately got off his horse and strapped his bull's-eye lanthorn to Nero's neck, for the light to shine behind. This was the very thing the dog seemed to want. Off he went, his master following him.

They had gone some miles like this, when Nero got *exceedingly fierce and excited*—and he was gone.

His master could hear nothing of him, or even see a glimmer of his lanthorn. All he heard was the bark of Nero a long distance off, as if he was in fierce fight, but he could not tell exactly which direction the sound came from.

The old lord rode about the wood, as well as his horse could get amongst the boughs and trees, until daylight began to set in, and was beginning to think the dog had been killed, when he noticed a lot of things scattered about a short distance off, and, on riding up, " Oh, what a sight met his eyes !"

There lay the wrecks of the gipsies tents. There lay a large bull-dog of the gipsies, " dead," and blood all about.

But nothing living was to be seen. The old
lord's heart sickened at the sight, and thought
nothing less than that he should soon see the dead
bodies of his child and dog.

There were all kinds of things lying about.
Even the large seething pot in which they cooked
their food; "and there laid Nero's bull's-eye
lanthorn."

At last he turned away, with a heavy heart, and
was about to leave the sickening scene, when he
thought he saw something more laying in some
bushes a short distance off, but this was but other
things similar to what he had already seen.

So he turned away, and at length got into a
narrow road, where the brambles, at places, grew
quite across it.

CHAPTER III.

E had gone down this some distance, when he beheld something, which he could form no idea of what it could be, but, as he got nearer, he at last beheld his noble dog, Nero, and his little son, getting along as well as they could.

The little fellow was leaning on the dog's neck, and the dog supporting him as well as he could.

His feet were much scratched with brambles, for the gipsies had taken off his boots. There was blood on his face, neck, and hands, which Nero continually licked off.

This blood was from a wound that Nero had received in his neck in his fearful fight with the gipsies.

When the fight began, Nero was near upon

L

loosing his young master, for Nero was attacked by a very fierce bull-dog of the gipsies, and could not get rid of him until he had fought and killed him.

Then the gipsy men came at Nero with knives, or anything they could get, but he tore them down so fast that, at last, they were glad to get away as best they could.

The last he had to attack was a strong, dark-faced gipsy man, who had got hold of the young lord and was getting him away, but Nero soon pulled him down, and it was then that he got his young master away.

The old lord jumped off his horse, and scarcely knew which to caress first, his son or the dog, so thankful was he.

He took his little son upon the horse, but he could see Nero was too weak to follow, so, with difficulty, he got him also upon the horse.

The weight was nothing to his horse, for it was a noble animal.

At last they got out of the wood, and, after a time, within sight of the castle (for they had to go very slowly), when they were seen by all the servants and people about the castle, who all came running to meet them.

When they had got before the castle door the excitement was very great.

A fair and beautiful lady ran with outstretched arms to receive the child. It was his MOTHER.

The wound in Nero's neck was well attended, as also the little fellow's bleeding feet, and soon all was well again.

From that time Nero and his young Master appeared better friends than before.

THE PRETTY YOUNG MAIDEN.

A pretty young maiden, her age was sixteen,
A fairer young maiden scarce ever was seen ;
Her father a jolly old farmer was he,
As long as the day just as happy was he.

He kept lots of pigs, also ducks and fat geese,
And cows that gave milk, which made butter and
  cheese ;
He also kept pigeons that fly in the air,
And so large were the eggs of his fowls, I declare.

His bees they made honey as fast as could be—
And sweeter fine honey you never did see ;
His orchards would often the branches bend down
With rosy-cheeked apples near touching the
  ground.

In spring all his meadows with cowslips looked
   gay,
In summer they yielded abundance of hay.
This jolly old farmer had also a wife,
And unknown to both was quarrel or strife.

The puddings she'd make in the course of a year
Were surprising to think of, I really declare;
Jams and jellies she made; also gooseberry wine,
Whoever did taste it declared it was fine.

In fact this old farmer lived a long life,
And shared all his plenty with daughter and wife.

RIGGER THE SAILOR.

A sailor who had served in the same ship for some years, and who was as good a sailor as ever sailed upon the foaming billows, being as great a favourite with the Captain as with the others engaged on board the ship. He had received the name of Rigger on account of his great agility in managing a ship in a heavy gale.

When the wind was blowing *great guns*, as the sailors call it, or the sea raging mountains high, at such times he was always up in the masts, altering the sails to suit every breeze, and had, consequently, many times saved the ship from the fearful calamity of foundering, when frequently all on board are lost.

"Rigger," said the Captain one day, "there is *one* thing out of *two* you must do; that is, you must leave the ship, or leave off drink, for you have been at least half your time drunk, and no use to me lately."

Rigger appeared somewhat surprised, and at last said, "Well, Cap'n, I shouldn't much like to leave you nor the ship, so I'd rather leave off the drink, no doubt I shall be able to get on as well without it in time."

"I am sure you would," said the captain.

"Then it's agreed," said Rigger, "no more of it for me."

"Give me your honest hand upon it," said the

captain, "and that's a better guarantee to me than all the pledge-signing in the country. Rigger gave the captain his hand, and both felt quite satisfied, for a better captain never had charge of a ship, nor a better sailor trod deck than Rigger when sober.

The ship sailed with a very valuable cargo, calling at the Cape of Good Hope, and thence on its long voyage.

CHAPTER II.

WHILST the ship was at the Cape, Rigger bought himself a book on Navigation, and studied it well, and was soon quite conversant with the sailing charts by which persons in charge of a ship know how to steer. After a time Rigger would often take upon himself to suggest to the captain that it would be better to " veer" a little more " sou-east or nor-west," and on referring to his own chart the captain generally found Rigger to be right.

The other sailors began by degrees to follow
Rigger's example, seeing how much happier and
better he appeared to be; and in time the good
ship arrived safely at London Docks with her
rich and valuable cargo.

After the unloading had taken place the captain called Rigger into his cabin to receive his
wages for the voyage out and back again, which
amounted to a great deal of money, for he had
not drawn any of it. The captain also made him
a handsome present for his exemplary conduct
and usefulness, which pleased him exceedingly.

"Shiver my topsails, said Rigger one day, "if
I don't go and see my poor old mother, for I
have not seen her for this three years and more."
The next morning off he started, and found his
mother had left the house in which Rigger was
born, and was living in the alms-houses, for she
could not afford to pay.the rent. This grieved
him very much; so after he had staid with her
a few days he began to think what he could do
towards his mother's happiness, and strolled along
the village to look at the house in which he was
born, to his agreeable surprise found it was

"To Let," upon which he immediately went and talked to the landlord, who agreed to sell him the house and garden, which Rigger, having sufficient money, gladly bought. It was only a day or two before Rigger's mother was again in her old loved home, free alike of landlord or rent.

THE LITTLE RAGGED BOY.

There was a little ragged boy
No shoes upon his feet,
All day he never went to school
But wandered in the street.

Once a happy home had he
With parents good and kind,
A happier little boy than he
Scarcely could you find.

His father and his mother died
Both within one year,
No money had they saved to keep,
Their little son so dear.

He wandered all about the streets
And slept where'er he could,
And often went all through the day
And scarcely tasted food.

One day he met a gentleman
Who spoke to him so kind,
And asked him how it was that he
No food or home could find.

Tho tears ran down his cheeks whilst he
　　Tho gentleman did tell,
Of his parents who were dead and gone,
　　By whom he was loved so well.

Come home with me my little man
　　And you shall quickly find
I'll buy you clothes and give you food,
　　And treat you very kind.

For when I was a little boy,
　　As near as I can tell,
My parents died as your's have done
　　Which I remember well.

I'll send you every day to school
　　If you will try and learn,
You may become as happy then
　　As now you are forlorn.

The little boy dried up his tears,
　　Right glad was he to find
That he had found a gentleman
　　Who was so good and kind.

M

THE MYSTERIOUS POEM.

The following "Poem," or by whatever name it may be designated, has been the subject of great speculation.

It appears to contain words used in the Italian, French, and Spanish languages, besides a slight smattering of Oriental dashed with Russio and Turkish jargon. Here and there an unmistakeable English word occurs.

It has also been affirmed by a gentleman who, whilst crossing the Mexican Praries, and who was taken captive by a tribe of wild Indians known as the "Pawnees," by whom he was held in captivity for a long time; Then there was war between them and a hostile tribe called the "Commanchee's," who captured and detained him over 30 moons.

This same gentleman states that during his captivities he pretty well understood the jargon or gibberish of both these wild and hostile tribes, and that he detects many words or sounds which are quite familiar to him as used by these wild and warlike people.

Nevertheless, many attempts have been made in order to convey an idea of its real purport, but the result has not proved quite harmonious, consequently we give the one which appears the best, and that the reader may find a greater facility, we give it *interversa*.

THE MYSTERIOUS POEM.

1. *Gondola do beso la zouch*
   Craponto lin bin van der ba
   Sinca to'edo cra vin
   Rotop mon ve le ra donra

1. If evil you wish for to do
   Your thoughts turn quickly away,
   Or perhaps you'll find out your mistake,
   If to evil you ever give way.

2. *Fil deca ramo mout rob*
  Singtola vil ren omer odrot
  Ilbana becon voke ent
  Gilkerena inbano ongrot.

2. Fortune's wheel turns rapidly round,
  Your prize may not yet be thrown up,
  It's perseverance that raises the man—
  *Gilkerena inbano ongrot.

  * This line has given immense trouble without *any* success.

3. *Pintalia crene quaffawee squa*
  Mendeno gib libba dren dwill
  Loman ind ona se quaff
  Caava glib glib dig ben-gil.

3. Repine not, O man, at thy state,
  God gives unto all as He will;
  From some He removeth the dross,
  Others He restraineth from ill.

4. *Spani prair gol lan mene*
  Tego raina don fide
  Clinquo vah-vah gol geran
  Mouche trop-na trop-ne del-ide.

4. To truth and simplicity cling,
   Virtue is a safe horse to ride,
   Fidelity follows her track,
   While prudence runs safe by her side.

5. *Bann moko fir vin da-ruch*
   Zabo ma-qua ven-vound
   Skilebo omena vah-vah
   Crolo quin-que va-vound

5. Be not enamoured too much
   With charms which beset thee around—
   Forsake not thy parents' advice
   And with honour your life shall be crown'd!

THE LIGHTERMAN'S DAUGHTER.

'Gainst Longstone's Rock that stormy night
  The sea beat fierce and strong;
How those waves lashed and foamed
  As in fury raged the storm.

The lighterman trembled as he lay in his bed,
  And that night was a stranger to sleep—
For experience had taught him sad lessons of men
  Being swallowed in that mighty deep.

But he was not alone—a fair daughter had he,
  Her eyes were both blue and bright—
She also had trembled for those on the deep
  On this fearful and desperate night.

At length the morn came, and, ere daylight had set,
　She took that old telescope long,
She scanned o'er the waters, she watched every speck,
　Her eyes wandered anxious and long.

"My father! my father!" in haste did she call,
　"A sad wreck I behold straight ahead,
They cling to the masts, whilst others they float
　Around seemingly numberless dead!

"Away, let's away, my father!" she said,
　"Our boat shall at once breast these waves;
By courage and strength in God's holy Name,
　This remnant we'll rescue from sad watery graves."

The old man in silence his aged head shook,
　"No human aid can avail;
Our small and frail bark is only a speck
　These lash-foaming waves to assail."

"Peace and courage, brave father," the maiden replied,
　"Of Grace Darling shall never be said
That her foot on the shore shall linger whilst life
　Is crying for help on the waves!"

Their small craft was launched 'mid the foam
　dashing waves,
　Whilst all hope of rescue seemed past,

But onward they went, never thinking that they
　Themselves might be leaving dry land for the last.

"We strain every muscle, brave father, pull strong,
　The wreck is before in full view.
They cling to the masts, they're exhausted—pull on;
　A few moments more and they all will be gone.

And now we are with them—we save one by one;
　And now they are all in our boat—
No, no, see that mother, high up in the mast,
　Senseless, tho' holding her child to her breast."

And now Grace bounds forth, leaving father and boat,
　Up the masts she ascends in sad haste;
She has rescued them both, thank God, they are saved
　From those foaming and maddening waves.

NEWCASTLE
WALTONIAN CLUB
Instituted
APRIL 5, 1822

Thomas Bewick.

THE GIANT AND GOLDEN KEY.

ONCE upon a time, a gentleman, with his little daughter, was passing through an orchard, when their attention was attracted by some beautiful apples on one of the trees, for they had never seen apples so immensely large or handsome before.

They were very much startled on hearing a very loud noise, and perceived an immense Giant coming towards them. The Giant, with slow, but

long strides, came straight to them, and, in a
tremendous voice, said, "What are you taking
my apples for?"

You may imagine how very frightened the little
girl and her father were.

The little girl's father said, "We were not taking your apples, sir."

The Giant gave a deep groan, and, taking the
little girl up with one hand, pointed to an immense apple, hanging very high, and told her to
take hold of it with both her hands, which, being
very frightened, she did.

As soon as she had got hold of the apple he
left his hold of her, and there she hung, clinging
to the apple. Soon, her weight brought the apple
from the tree, but the Giant had not taken his
great eyes off, so he caught her in his hands.

He next went to a tree which was almost breaking down with plums of a beautiful purple colour,
and very large.

He shook the tree with his immense strength,
and the plums fell upon the ground as thick as
hailstones falling in a storm.

He then told the little girl's father to pick them

up and put them in his pockets, but there was enough to fill fifty pockets. So the Giant took from his own pocket a handkerchief as large as a table cloth, and told him to put the others in that.

. Then said the Giant to the gentleman, " Whoso little girl is this ?"

The gentleman said, " Mine, sir."

" Have you any more at home ?" the Giant said.

" Five more," said the gentleman.

The giant gave a loud and deep groan. Then, after a little while, he said, " Take the plums to your children at home, but this little girl I will take with me." So saying, he took her upon his shoulder, gave a deep groan, and walked away with her.

CHAPTER II.

HEN the Giant got to his Castle he was holding the little girl still upon his shoulder, and, with his fist, struck three times at the Castle gates. Two immense gates were immediately opened by two men, who were servants to the Giant. As soon as the Giant had gone in the gates were closed.

The Giant then put the little girl upon the ground, took hold of her hand, and led her into the Castle.

Every one must imagine how very frightened the little girl would be; and so she was. She was even so frightened that she was afraid to cry.

On the Giant went, leading her through a long

passage, and then opened a door into a very large room.

. In this room there was a beautiful dinner on the table. The Giant took her and placed her in a chair at the table, and sat down himself. He then cut her some dinner, "about enough for two men," and began to eat his own. When he looked up, and noticed she was not eating— the reason of which was that the knife and fork was larger than a carving knife and fork—the Giant gave a deep sigh, and told his servants to go and fetch one smaller.

After the meat was taken away, there were puddings and pies, and many very nice things. The little girl, seeing so many nice things, was pleased, and ate a good dinner, which greatly pleased the Giant.

The Giant then took her in his lap, but as she happened to look up in his face she saw great tears running down his checks, and heard him give a deep groan, which surprised her very much.

The reason of this was, the Giant had once had a daughter of his own, who had died a short time before, and he was so fond of her that he could

N

not bear to live in his Castle with only servants.
He told her all about his daughter. Now the
little girl had not once spoken to the Giant, because she was so frightened; but, when the Giant
had done telling her about his own little daughter
that was dead, she looked up in his face and said,
"What was her name, Mr. Giant?"

The Giant told her it was "Miranda," and
asked her if she would like to be called by that
name. She said, as it was a very pretty name,
she should, which pleased him very much.

CHAPTER III.

THEN the Giant got up and took Miranda by the hand, and went along some passages in the Castle until he came to a great door. He then took out of his pocket a "GOLDEN KEY," and unlocked the door.

All along one side were a number of milk-white horses, very beautiful to look at.

The Giant appeared very pleased to show them to Miranda, but there was something on the other side that pleased her much better, which was four beautiful milk-white ponies.

Miranda knew, as soon as she saw them, that they had belonged to the Giant's daughter, so she did not ask him.

He took her to them, and, when he saw how wonderfully pleased she was in looking at them, he asked her if she would like one to call her own.

At first, she thought he could not mean it, but

when she looked in his face she was sure he did, so she said, "Yes, Mr. Giant."

"Very well then," he said ; "choose which you like best." But they were all so handsome, she did not know which to choose.

At last she decided on one. Then the Giant told one of his servants to take it to a very pretty little stable, which he did ; "But," said the Giant, "it will be dull by itself. It must have company." So he said, "Choose again."

Miranda was so surprised that she could scarcely believe it true ; so she looked up in his face and said, in a very low voice, almost a whisper, "I would rather you choose the other, Mr. Giant."

Of all the things she could have said to the Giant to please him, was just what she did say, and, for the first time, the Giant smiled and seemed pleased. Miranda had never seen him smile before, and she was very glad, for she knew that he grieved for his little daughter that was dead.

Then the Giant went up to one of the ponies patted and tickled it, at which the pony appeared as pleased as possible, for the Giant's horses and ponies all were very fond of him, because he was so kind to them.

The Giant had not driven his milk-white horses since his daughter's death. He had never once hit them with a whip, because they knew his voice and were always ready and glad to do more for him in love than he ever could have made them do through fear. He well knew that it spoiled horses to "whip them." So he unfastened it, put her on its back, and led it to the little stable where her other pony was.

He then showed her a very pretty little carriage and harness for the ponies, which he also gave her.

CHAPTER IV.

MIRANDA soon made herself quite at home, and could find her way about the Castle.

She had plenty to amuse her, for there were several large boxes of beautiful playthings.

One day the Giant said to her, " Should you like to go and see your father and mother, and your brothers and sisters ?"

" I should very much like to go, Mr. Giant," she said.

· " But, if I let you go, you will not come back again," he said.

" Oh, I am sure I will, Mr. Giant. I like being here."

" Very well," the Giant said, " To-morrow, you shall go."

So, on the next day, the Giant told one of his servants to make the two ponies which he had given to Miranda look very nice, put the harness on, and put them in the pony carriage. He then got a large basket and put in it a very large pie, a plum pudding, and a lot of nice things ; he also told her to take some playthings for her brothers and sisters. Then the Giant lifted her up into the pony carriage and gave her the reins, and, just as she was going to drive off, he said " *Stay*." He went away, and, in a few moments, returned with a bag in one of his hands, which appeared very heavy. This he put in the carriage, and told her not to forget and give it to her father.

She then gave him a kiss, the gates were thrown open, and off she dashed.

No little girl could be more pleased than she was, as she sat in her little carriage, with the ponies trotting as fast as possible, swishing their tails as they went along.

After a while, she turned down the road that led to her father's house.

Her brothers and sisters were at play in the garden in front of the house, and, when they saw her a long way off, ran in and told their father and mother that a fine young lady was driving down the road, with such a lovely pair of white ponies and a carriage, little thinking it was their own sister. But, to their surprise, she pulled up

in front of the gate, jumped out, kissed all her
brothers and sisters, and then ran into the house
to her father and mother, who were so surprised
that they could scarcely believe their own eyes.

"Oh, dear! Oh, dear," they all said. "We
thought the nasty old Giant had killed and eaten
you up."

But she said, "Oh, no. He is a very good
Giant." At which they were all very much
surprised.

She then ran back to the carriage and lifted the toys out, at the sight of which they were all delighted. Then the servant lifted out the large plum pudding and pie, and all were as pleased as possible; and she told them all about the Giant's Castle, and how good he was to her. So, after she had been there some time, she said she must go back, as the Giant would be expecting her.

Then, when her brothers and sisters heard all this, they wanted to go and see the Giant, but she said she would give them a nice ride instead, and, just as she was putting them into the carriage, she saw the heavy bag that the Giant had put in for her father. But it was so heavy he could scarcely carry it into the house, but when he opened it he found it was a bag of " bright sovereigns," at which he was never so pleased in his life before.

Miranda brought her brothers and sisters back after giving them a nice ride, and after kissing her father and mother about twenty times each, drove back to the Castle, where she found the Giant at the gate waiting for her.

CHAPTER V.

MIRANDA had now been in the Castle a long time, and the Giant had been kind to her, but still she could not help feeling great surprise as to how the Castle and all within it were maintained, for there appeared to her great mystery respecting it. She had always noticed what special care the Giant exercised in the use of the *Golden Key*, and would never allow her to come near him whilst he used it, and with what care he placed it—not in his pocket—but in his bosom.

It chanced one day that, after carefully locking a door, the key accidentally fell from his hand upon the floor. Miranda sprang towards it, and was about to stoop to pick it up in order to give it him, when—to her surprise—he called out with a voice that shook that part of the Castle, which so frightened her that she could scarcely stand, and, feeling ill, asked the Giant, when it got dark, if she might go to her bed, which he allowed her to do; but when she had got to bed she could not sleep, and began to feel so frightened that she wished to leave the Castle and the Giant who had so frightened her, and she thought of her father and mother and brothers and sisters and began to wish she was again with them, and there she laid until the Castle great clock had struck twelve at midnight.

As soon as the clock had finished striking, she saw a door open out of the wall of her room, and twenty little fairies, all bearing tapers of different coloured lights, followed each other into the room. They made no noise, but commenced dancing and waving their tapers very gracefully. After they had danced some time, they stood in a circle, and the door in the wall again opened, when a fairy more beautiful and also larger came, bearing a torch with appearance resembling a beautiful fountain, and the rays of light that shot forth from it appeared like hundreds of blended colours, too beautiful to imagine without seeing.

As soon as this fairy entered, she was received with great rejoicing, and immediately entered the circle, when the others all waved their torches around her. Then the twenty fairies gently approached her, and she raised her wand or torch towards the ceiling, when one of the twenty fairies in an instant ascended with her torch and touched the ceiling, and a table of sparkling crystal descended, upon which were all kinds of dainties.

They sat upon sparkling seats, which appeared supported without touching the floor. After they had all taken as much as they pleased, the fairy again raised her torch of many colours, and the table of crystal ascended whilst another descended, laden with choicest fruits, and wines of the greatest delicacies, besides balms and choice perfumes more delicate than the morning dew.

After this they danced many dances known only to fairies. They also sang many sweet songs, the words of which were quite unintelligible, except the chorus, which was—

> Who of this Castle would be free,
> First must touch the *Golden Key!*

Then there was an immense noise made by the Giant below, who was in great trouble at having let the key touch the floor, for he was afraid harm would come on account of it.

Upon hearing this noise, all the faries disappeared through the door in the wall by which they came.

Miranda was so astonished at all this, that she scarcely could realise it, and then she thought,

why, this must be a Castle of Enchantment, and
it was nearly daylight before she could sleep, and
even them dreamed of the fairies until she awoke
in the morning.

As soon as she awoke she rubbed her eyes and
did not appear to understand where she was.
After a time she stood upon a high chair and
looked out of one of the Castle windows, and even
then she could not understand where she was; at
length, at a long distance off, she saw two boys
with a donkey, and then she knew she must be
awake.

o

CHAPTER VI.

The Giant appeared very much troubled, and scarcely took any notice of Miranda, for he was quite different to what he had been, instead of being glad to see her, her presence seemed to trouble him, and she could not imagine how different everything in the Castle now was, nor how to account for it, and yet it seemed to her that the dropping of the Golden Key was the cause, and yet how small a circumstance it appeared just the dropping of a key, but if she had known then as much as she did shortly after, she would have understood more about it.

It had often astonished Miranda very much that, although there was an abundance of everything in the Castle, even to the choicest dainties, yet she never saw anyone come there, for none could come to the Castle, or leave it without the Giant, for it was the same Golden Key that locked and unlocked every door.

After this Miranda laid awake night after night, and rarely could get sleep until daylight began to peep into her room, which was not much, for the windows in that Castle were very small; and so time went on, and Miranda began to get very melancholy and sad. One night she was, as usual, laying awake, when a faint light began to illumine the room; it was not the kind given by ordinary lights, but, besides being very much more brilliant, there was a softened influence blended as if by numerous different colours, which made it appear as singular as charming. Then after a short time a door opened from the wall (not that by which she had seen the twenty-one fairies enter and depart, but on the opposite side of the room), then a number of small fairies entered and formed themselves into a row on each side, they each had a sparkling light on their forehead which shone with great brilliancy. After they were arranged in order, there was a soft noise as if many beautiful voices were approaching, and soon more fairies entered, bearing a chair which sparkled like diamonds; in the chair was the form of a beautiful woman, but not so large. She was

habited all in black—blacker than could be imagined; in her girdle she had a key which was
also blacker than ebony. As soon as she alighted
from her chair she waved her hand to the fairies
to depart by the way they came and in the same
order. By the brilliancy of the light Miranda
could not help noticing that the arm she waved
was black, whilst the other was as white as snow ;
it was also the same with her long flowing hair,
one half was dead black whilst the other was
snowy white. As soon as her fairy attendants
had all departed she appeared as if in the act of
listening for some time, then as if quite satisfied
that all was still, she slowly approached the bed
upon which Miranda was.

Miranda's heart now beat fast, and she scarcely
breathed. After again listening for some time,
the form addressed Miranda thus :—" I have
known you from the day you were brought to
this Castle, and my ever watchful eye has been
upon you, although you knew it not. This Castle
exists by enchantment, and it had always been
mine, until by a circumstance too singular to be
believed, the present Giant was allowed to reign

here, but the brightness of his reign is now past, and even fast on the wane. You will not be surprised to hear that all the splendour and wealth of this enchanted Castle is subject to the one who possesses the Golden Key. The Giant who brought you here at that time possessed all the power the key was capable of bestowing, but one half has lately gone from him. This key and its powers are not even now fully known, for it is supposed that a combination of all good fairies has conferred upon it more power than one possessor could be capable of using.

" There are great mysteries attached to the use of this key, one of which is that when it is once fully in any one's possession, it must be touched by no other hand, or its power as well as itself, to them is once and for ever gone.

" The Giant who so lately held it entire has now lost its half; that loss was occasioned by his so completely letting it fall, and in which you so innocently sprang to pick up to restore to his hand; behold this hand, its whiteness is complete; see this silken hair, and the entire of myself was as black as deepest night until that

golden key fell upon the floor; before that I had
no power to touch it even had opportunity ·
offered; now opportunity is all I require, for I
have now power to take it even in my hand—
this hand of whiteness, and then by touching
with this enchanted golden key this hand of
blackness and the other half of myself will be
restored even like to the other, and all my former
splendour and beauty will be restored and completed."

Then there was a curious kind of noise in
another part of the Castle, and the half-fairy
hastily telling Miranda she would visit her again
soon, was gone.

CHAPTER VII.

MIRANDA now saw very little of the Giant, and only as he wandered about the Castle in a very strange manner, for he could not rest, and was also heard about at different times in the night, for he appeared to be sensible of the fate that was awaiting him through dropping the key.

It was only a few nights after when Miranda was laying awake as usual, that soft lights began to appear in her room, and in a moment the door from the wall again opened.

The twenty fairies appeared as before with their lights of many colours, and then appeared the black-white fairy. This time she sat upon a horse most grandly caparisoned, but the horse was from the half of his face, straight along his back, and even to the half of his flowing tail, the one side dead black and the other snow white, and the contrast was most striking. As soon as the black-white fairy had alighted she waved her white arm in which she carried her torch of many colours, and the horse and other smaller fairies disappeared as they came.

Then the fairy lifted her arm of jet black, and looking at it gave a long and deep sigh; then she appeared as if in the act of listening, and appearing satisfied she heard no noise, cautiously approached the bed of Miranda.

Miranda was not so surprised this time as before, although the appearance of the fairy was very surprising, for straight from the parting of her hair, down one side of the face was snow white, whilst the other was jet black, her long flowing hair on each side being in black and white contrast.

" Miranda," said the fairy, " according to my promise I visit you again ; you now have it in your power to render me services to which all the wealth in this Castle would be as nothing if you will comply with my wishes.

" I will, in as few words as possible, inform you of what I would have you do, for it is not only in your power to restore me to my former loveliness (here the fairy held up her snow white arm, looked upon it for some time with evident delight, after which she looked upon the other of jet black, and gave a deep sigh) but you will give me also the power of conferring upon you —here the fairy paused and listened for awhile : then continuing, she said—" Know that I am descended from a long and noble race of fairies who have from time to time held uncontrolled possession of the ' Charmdelor,' or what is now called the Golden Key, the properties of which have been for thousands of years known only to us, but the knowledge of many of its great powers have departed, but to me alone descends the mysteries capable of being amply and efficiently used by one fairy.

" The Giant, who so lately held it entire, but who has, through so carelessly allowing it to fall upon the floor of its own Castle, never ought to have had any possession of it; nevertheless, he has proved himself unworthy of holding so great a gift, and now is the time for me to exercise everything in my power in order to gain its possession. Therefore, you are the only one who has full access to every part of this Castle, and it is to you I trust to enable me to get it;

but know this Key is enclosed in a magic box profusely inlaid with charms, the opening of which is known only to the Giant and myself. You are aware that in the day he carries it in his bosom, at night it is always under the pillow upon which his head rests, and it is this that I want you to assist me in getting. You must steal softly (as the clock strikes the midnight hour) into his chamber, and assuring yourself that he is sleeping, with your small hand gently withdraw it from under his head and bring it to me to a part of the Castle that I will tell you, and this is the service you must do me, for I myself must not approach the breath of the Giant. I shall then, when in possession of this great and long coveted gift, show you I am capable of rewarding your services."

Footsteps were now heard wandering about the Castle, and the fairy was gone.

CHAPTER VIII.

No sooner had the fairy departed than the door opened and the Giant entered Miranda's room; he had no light, but the moon shone brightly through the latticed window. Miranda could just observe by the moon's light that he was carrying in his hand something which sparkled with great brilliancy, and she concluded it must be the box containing the Golden Key. He did not appear to notice that he was in Miranda's room, for after wandering about for some time he departed.

Soon after this Miranda fell asleep and then dreamed. She dreamed that in a far distant part of the country there was a valley of great extent, surrounded by immense high rocks and mountains, and that no one had ever been to it, and that the people who inhabited it thought there was no more world than that, nor any other people beside themselves; and she also dreamed that in this valley, which was called Partan, or the Happy

Valley, were thousands of waggon loads of diamonds and precious stones, for which the people cared nothing, as there was an abundance of other precious things of greater value and beauty. That fruits and greater luxuries were in that valley, such as were known in no other kingdom.

She also dreamed that the inhabitants of the Happy Valley had even more than they could wish for, and that none of them were ever ill or sad, and knew nothing but happiness, except in one thing, and that was that it had been foretold by many generations of the people in the Happy Valley that a Prince of their own people should refuse to take a wife of the virgins of the happy valley, and that he should cause great uneasiness to the inhabitants, for he would exercise all the great wealth and power at his command to find another world from which he could choose him a wife.

Miranda was disturbed in her beautiful dream by the rays of the sun shining full upon her, and she awoke.

CHAPTER IX.

DAY by day everything in the Castle was fast
fading away, and the Giant's state of mind became
quite alarming to behold. Miranda was quite
sensible that it was of no use trying to escape, as
the Giant had lost all use of the Key, and the
Castle gates were secure against any power that
could be brought against them, unless by the full
power of the Key. Miranda began almost to think
herself a prisoner in the Castle rather than living
there, and she was determined to search about
the Castle to ascertain if she could discover any
unknown outlet by which she could escape. In
order to accomplish this, she wandered through
many curious rooms, some of which appeared not
to have been used for a length of time.

One day, as she was in a part of the Castle she
had not been in before she noticed a very curious
figure attached to the wall which appeared exceedingly old and in the form of a picture, but
instead of being painted as she had seen pictures,
the colours appeared to be worked by a needle

P

with gold and silver threads; never having seen anything of its kind before she stood and examined it very minutely, and was soon able to discover that it was intended to represent some very important personage. She stood for a long time very intently admiring the great care and fine artistic labour which had been bestowed upon it, and being anxious to see as much of its beauties as were still in preservation, she gently moved it in order to obtain a more perfect view, when something fell from behind it upon the floor. This she picked up, and after having examined it found it was a number of fine skins of animals sewn so neatly together that she was scarcely able to see the joining.

The skins contained some writing, and in places she could scarcely make out what the writing meant, as it appeared to have been written hundreds of years, and some of the letters were made different to what she had seen before. The writing was also written in red.

Miranda sat down upon the floor, and after looking at it for a long time she was able to read and understand what it was about.

And this was the reading—

"A short history of the surprising life and death of the Emperor Ben Eni Ben Kick written with his own blood."

There was a mighty ruler named Ben Eni Ben Kick; he was held in great dread by all his subjects, for when he was wroth he would do unto them very cruel things. He called all his subjects together, and said unto them, "It hath come to my knowledge that you drink wine, and also indulge in luxuries such as only rulers should enjoy, therefore I charge all you my subjects that you drink no more wine even on pain of death." And the people looked upon Ben Eni Ben Kick and were greatly afraid.

Then the people said, "We will obey thee in all things only take not our wine from us."

At this Ben Eni's wrath became very great; then the people with a loud voice, louder than was ever heard in any land, gave ninety cheers for the great Ben Eni Ben Kick, and the ground was reddened with blood, for great numbers broke blood vessels in so loud cheering.

When Ben Eni Ben Kick heard the loudness of

his subjects' cheering he was somewhat appeased, more especially when he beheld the blood coming from the mouths of them that had overcheered themselves. Then he said, "Your voices have sounded in mine ears, but my commands must receive some appeasing." He held in his hand a spear, and raised it, and thrust it through the body of one of his subjects who stood nearest to him. Then he appeared a little appeased, and his subjects a great deal more frightened.

Ben Eni Ben Kick had given great study as to the most severe mode of torturing his subjects, and had arrived at very fair perfection in that way.

Ben Eni Ben Kick, though great in power, was small in stature ; he was also very plump, and he thought, in order to frighten his subjects still more, he would show them something new, and he looked well around him, and beheld a man sitting upon the ground suitable to his purpose, for the man was one of those who had over-cheered themselves, and consequently felt very ill.

With great dignity, Ben Eni Ben Kick ap-

proached the man and looked well around to see
that he was observed by all his subjects; then
did he look well to what he was about to do; he
took good aim with his foot and with one tremendous kick did he kick, but the man had in-
stinctively disobeyed by suddenly lowering his
head just at the time he ought not; consequently
Ben Eni's toes found no resistance, and higher
than his head into the air they went, and his
body lost its equilibrium, and he came down upon
his head with great force and broke his neck.

When his subjects saw that he was dead they
were immediately inspired with great courage,
and each gave him a kick.

Then they said, " Let us away to his palace
and taste his tap," and to his palace they went.
When they had entered his palace they found his
cellars so well stocked with vintages of every
kind that every one had as much as they would.

His palace also contained very great treasures
of gold and precious things.

They found also that Ben Eni Ben Kick had
also managed to smuggle into his palace thirty
wives, which he kept there.

They released the thirty wives, and sold all the treasures and divided equally to every man, and they destroyed the palace, and would from that time become subject to no other ruler, for they had received sufficient thereof, even of the ruling of Ben Eni Ben Kick.

CHAPTER X.

MIRANDA was so interested in the reading about Ben Eni Ben Kick that she did not observe that the light of day was fast fading away, but after . she had read it all she still held it in her hand, and she looked at the portrait of needlework and thought it must be meant for Ben Eni Ben Kick, then a sort of drowsiness came over her and she fell asleep.

The great clock of the Castle struck the midnight hour, and Miranda awoke. She could not for some time understand where she was, for all was darkness, then suddenly she remembered about Ben Eni Ben Kick. She felt about the room, but could not find the door by which she entered, for there were long ranges of rooms leading to each other, and after trying for a long time, feeling round the walls, she at length became so confused that she had not the least idea which way to try, and at the same

moment she saw the black-white fairy coming towards her with her torch of many colours.
Miranda felt somewhat alarmed, although at the
same time she was glad, because she thought
there was no cause for being afraid.   On the fairy
came, and was going past where Miranda stood,
but the glare of the torch of many colours shed so
bright a ray upon her face, the fairy noticed it
and stopped, then, after raising the torch to throw
a more powerful light fully upon her, the fairy
stood for a moment, and approaching her said,

" And what is the cause that you are here alone
at the midnight hour ? "

· " Good fairy," said Miranda, " I slept, and it is
thus that I am here."

" Fear nothing," said the fairy, " this my
purpose suits full well, for

> " Ere this dull earth again the sun shall see,
> This hand shall grasp the golden key."

Here the fairy raised her hand of snowy whiteness
and bade Miranda follow her.   She led her
through long avenues of the Castle, and at length
came to a door, before which the fairy listened
with great care, then, after a short pause,

"He sleeps," said the fairy. "It is now in your power to possess me of more than tongue can tell and more than mind can conceive. I have told thee, Miranda, that I know how to acknowledge services; enter, and take from beneath his sleeping head

"All that power to me can give."

At this moment there was an immense shock, such as of an earthquake, and the foundations of the Castle seemed to tremble. The fairy caught Miranda up, and conveyed her to her chamber with great haste.

The next moment the Giant had stumbled from within his room, and scarcely appeared to understand what he was about to do—he descended the great stairs as if in the act of encountering a foe.

It was now that the fairy, with eyes sparkling and her whole frame trembling with agitation, made the bold venture of which, to her, was annihilation or great power. She approached the bed upon which the Giant's form had only a moment before been reposing. For a moment, and only a moment, she sought and had obtained possession of the box in which was contained all her existence desired, when the Giant hastily returned, and beholding the black-white fairy; with desperation seized a sword of great length which always hung near his head, the edge of which was sharper than razors newly set, and raising it high above his head was about to cleave the fairy from head to foot, when she succeeded in touching the magic spring, and the box with lightning rapidity flew open!

The lightning from the skies could not have been more rapid than the movements which the black-white fairy exercised in obtaining possession of the key with her fairy hand of snowy whiteness, and ere the Giant's sword had fallen upon her to cleave her in two, she had touched with the magic key her arm of blackness, and the magic charm its work had done, for the Giant's hand relaxed its hold, and the sword upon the floor fell!

The Giant stood without the power to move or speak.

The fairy then in all her restored beauty (for her blackness departed at the touch of the magic key) addressed the Giant in these words:—

This key you might have held supreme
    Till time's remotest day ;
Your hour is past, your power is gone—
    Your rule has passed away.

The fairy then with her foot stamped upon the floor, and in a loud voice called out, OBEY! Immediately the room was filled with lights of great brilliancy, and fairies appeared in great beauty and splendour. The black-white horse also appeared and stood behind her, which no sooner had the fairy touched than it was changed entirely to the purest whiteness and great beauty.

Then the fairy looked upon the Giant, who stood without power to move or speak, and addressed him thus:

"Since a combination of all the great fairy charms have bestowed such power upon the magic key, no possessor has so slighted the use of its power as you, who have now lost for ever all the great and mighty gifts it is capable of bestowing, and now what is left for me is to destroy your existence. Nevertheless, there is one in this Castle to whom you once showed kindness, and for that your existence shall continue amongst

your own species, where you shall live, therefore
understand—

"I banish you to Giantland!"

And the huge form of the giant instantaneously
disappeared. Then they danced a fairy dance
and sung—

> We of this Castle are now all free,
> And our Queen possesses the Golden Key!

CHAPTER XI.

THE Fairy Queen now exercised the magic power of the Golden Key, and not only extended the size of the Castle, but furnished it with great magnificence, so that

> If all the fairies in the land
> Could exercise their magic wand,
> No greater charms could e'er be seen
> Produced by power of Fairy Queen!

The Fairy Queen had taken care · to supply Miranda with the choicest luxuries, and now visited her to enquire what services she should render her, thinking she would desire to be made a fairy and share the delights of fairy life, but the request that Miranda made was, that she should be permitted to see the Prince of the Happy Valley.

"There is nothing," replied the Queen of the Golden Key, "but what I am capable of granting, therefore your desire shall be fulfilled."

And with that she left Miranda and departed, and commanded one of her fairies to visit, with

Q

great haste, the Happy Valley, and appear to the
Prince of that Valley, and cause him to dream
that the prophecy of the inhabitants for so many
ages of the Happy Valley must now or never be
fulfilled, and that the virgin whom he must wed
was awaiting him, and that her wealth was equal
to all the great outlay of fortune to which he
would be subject in order to leave the Happy
Valley to come and claim her for his wife, and
then he must conduct her in great state and pomp
along the kingdoms of people through which he
must pass.

As soon as the Prince of the Happy Valley had dreamed this dream his impatience knew no bounds. He ordered all the men of might and honour to assemble, and instructed them with haste to continue the great opening which had for many years been carried on through a rock, to find a passage whereby the Prince was to proceed in order to obtain the virgin whom it had been prophecied he should receive for his wife. The height of this tunnel was fifty feet, and the width was ninety feet, for it was prophecied that the Prince should return with great pomp and splendour.

Then the men of might and honour made all preparation to continue the tunnel, and a thousand men worked by day and a thousand also by night, and in six hundred and sixty days they had continued the tunnel under the rock which surrounded the Happy Valley, and the length of the tunnel was twenty and four miles, and they continued incessantly by night and by day, and in eleven days more they had—to their great joy—succeeded in their great undertaking, and had entered, through the rock, into another country.

As soon as this was done, they made every possible haste to inform their prince, who ordered great numbers of the highest people in the Valley to prepare to accompany him, and in forty days all were in readiness.   The rocky tunnel was

lighted throughout with lamps of great magnificence. Costly tents in which to repose by night were also prepared, and also the luxuries of the Happy Valley in great abundance, and they started with great rejoicings.

The prince rode in a magnificent car, drawn by four animals of great strength and beauty; his attendants also appeared in great splendour.

They were all very much interested with the different places through which they passed, and also with the people, for all was quite different from what they had ever seen.

CHAPTER XII.

" Now," said the fairy, " in a few days the Princo of the Happy Valley will be here to entreat you to be his wife. We must prepare for him more magnificence than he has ever seen; all this I will do for you, and greater things should you consent to become Queen of the Happy Valley."

In a few days, as the Prince continued on his journey, he beheld the Castle, which answered in

every way to the one he had seen in his dreams, therefore he went towards it, and was greatly astonished at its outward grandeur, but more so when he had been admitted, for the fairy had left nothing which would add to the grandeur and magnificence of the mode in which she intended to entertain him. The Prince and those by whom he was attended had seen nothing but their own valley, so they were greatly surprised at the way in which they were received at the Castle.

After the Prince had communicated to the fairy his reason for visiting the Castle, she informed him that he had so far been successful, and that the virgin whom he sought to take for his wife was then within the Castle where he now was. Upon this the Prince expressed great anxiety to see her immediately, but the fairy told him she was preparing to appear before him, and that in ten days his wishes should be complied with and he should see her.

The Prince thought ten days a very long time, but felt great joy at being so fortunate as to find the Castle in which she was. So the fairy enter-

R

tained him and all those who were with him until the ten days had expired.

During this time the fairies had been preparing the choicest and most valued things it was possible to imagine for Miranda to appear in before the Prince of the Happy Valley, and when he saw her he was so surprised at her beauty and riches that all his expectations were greatly surpassed.

Then there were great rejoicings in the Castle, and the Prince asked Miranda to go with him and be the Queen of the Happy Valley, to which she

consented, and after more rejoicings they departed with great joy, for the fairy had sent Miranda away in great splendour.

When they arrived at the Happy Valley there

was very great gladness, and soon all the arrange-
ments were completed for the marriage of Miranda
and the Prince, which took place amidst great
and prolonged rejoicings throughout the Happy
Valley!

TALLY-HO!

TATTEN TATTEN'S FIRST FOX HUNT.

No boy with greater courage at the age of sixteen
ever crossed a horse than Tatten Tatten ; in fact
you would think by the masterly manner in which
he managed that animal, that he really must have
been born on horseback. But it is not so surprising when considered that he descended from
that line of ancestors who, from generation to
generation, were not only the proprietors of, as it
were, a perpetual pack of hounds, but also spared

no trouble or expense in the animals who were to carry them in their recreations of the excitement of the chase.

In the present age much has been written about the nervous system, but the generations of Tattens, like most fox-hunters, never knew that they were troubled with nerves, only such as were required in riding at something formidable which required great nerve and skill to successfully get their horse as well as themselves through.

Young Tatten had not only been familiar with the association of red-coats and long-lash hunting whips, but he had also listened with childish eagerness to the relation of exciting runs, desperate feats of horsemanship achieved, and all those excitements incidental to a good day's hunting, and had often within himself, as he bestrode his rocking-horse, longed for the time to come when he, too, should share in the healthful sport.

But time went on, and, as we have said, found Tatten in his sixteenth year, and then it was that he was permitted to mount for his first hunt.

It was with feverish excitement that he sprang from his bed, as most young sportsmen do who

are privileged to share the joys of a good day's
hunt, and he was not a little encouraged to behold
a "cloudy sky and southern wind," necessary to a
good day's run.

Old Moody, the huntsman, mounted upon his
favourite mare, both of which knew the country
—every hedge and ditch—within a radius of forty
miles, was in high spirits to witness, for the first
time, the young heir of so many generations and
patrons of the old English sport.

"My opinion," said Moody, "has been formed of him before the time he was old enough to say my name, and he will show us one day that he is worthy of the name of his forefathers."

It was an imposing sight—"that meet." The
proudest of England's aristocracy down to the
small farmer were well represented. Ladies in
the first blossom of youth and beauty, with smiling faces and graceful forms, appeared equally
impatient to display their courage and equestrian
accomplishments.

"We will try the gorse first," suggested the
huntsman ; "it never failed a fox yet. High in
boys ; find him. Hark, Tuner, hark!

" WHAR HARE, NORA, WHAR HARE."

Not too forward with that grey horse, sir ;
you're ahead of the dogs. Hoick ! hoick !"

Many of the dogs, as if clearing their throats for readiness, gave tongue more or less, but still the work of systematic trying went on in a thoroughly acknowledged way until a slight whimper from one of the dogs was heard. This would not have been noticed by any not intimately acquainted with that noble pack, but no sooner was that slight whimper given, than the heads of huntsmen, whipper-in, and all the dogs were raised, listening for a confirmation of the same; in a moment or two it was repeated, upon which every dog dashed to the spot.

"Hark! Gaylass, hark!" simultaneously echoed huntsman and whipper-in.

"She's unkennelled him, Tom," shouted the former, and at the same time the music of the pack burst upon the ear excitingly harmonious. The impatient and well-fed steeds were, if possible, more impetuous than their riders.

Away went Reynard with outstretched brush, in the full flower of foxhood, at a racing pace amidst the shouts of "Tally-ho!" as if bent upon showing them of what stuff he was made.

He makes a straight run across country for
Newton Copse, crosses the three-mile bottom,
dashes down the mill stream as far as the Forge

farm, breaks towards the three chimneys, makes
straight through Hedginford Thicket, crosses

Netly bottom, taking a straight course for Stoney Field's level.

The dogs were running with their noses breast high; on looking on from a distance, one would have imagined they were viewing their game, but it was not so, the scent was so good that they had not the trouble of picking it up.

The soil was heavy, the pace killing, yet the
noble steeds steadied down to their work in stately
order. A young lady with golden hair flying in
careless grace over her shoulders, displayed some
fine feats of horsewomanship by clearing hedges,
gates, and ditches as they came in her way.

It was now that the jaded steeds began, more
or less, to show signs of distress, when an unex-
pected double of Reynard changed the whole
aspect of affairs. Taking a circuit of Headley
Heath, the pack was now in *full view*, and now

was the exciting time for those who had bravely held out for the finish—another hundred yards and they will run into him! no, he doubles again, makes for the brook, crosses the road over the hill field—another ten minutes and he will be done—his brush is dragging the ground, and the music of the pack is exciting in the extreme. Now the last effort, and the dogs are upon him, and the brush—the coveted trophy—is in the hands of young Tatten Tatten!

STORY OF THE MERCHANT.

A MERCHANT who had started in business with a capital so small that would not have been sufficient to purchase an ass to assist him in carrying his stuffs, seeing that he had nothing to depend upon but industry and self-denial, lost no opportunity of acquiring a position in the world which would relieve him from the cares and anxieties necessary to those who have nothing but their own exertions to depend upon.

It mattered little to him what obstacles presented themselves, but he would attack them with such resolution, that he appeared easily to remove them. He was often heard to say, "Give me difficulties, and I will surmount them; but give me difficulties," and in process of time he increased his business so extensively that he found himself possessed of great wealth.

Now, said he, I am capable of well providing for children, if God should add that blessing to

so many others that he has bestowed upon me.
So with great care he sought a woman who
might add to his happiness, and make him a
good wife, and at length decided upon one whom
he imagined would be all he desired. At first
they lived happily, and contributed greatly to
each other's happiness, but his wife, finding that
her husband's wealth was much greater than she
imagined, and that he did not live up to his
income, she grew petulant, and even neglected
her attire when at home, but when she went
abroad nothing was sufficiently costly for her.

If her husband wished her to accompany him,
it was always irksome to her, and she never
cared to go at such times, although he had not
only been at considerable expense, but great
personal inconvenience.

He exercised great discretion in the choice of
friends, and preferred those of more solid worth
to such as professed great grandeur and slight
means. On the contrary, his wife was fond of
frivolity, and the more she opposed her husband,
the more she considered herself justified. And
time went on until he became weary of his wife,
and she soon died.

After a reasonable time, he again sought a
wife, and at length succeeded in finding such as
he thought would not be subject to the follies of
the one whom he had lost, for he took her from

indigent and placed her in affluent circumstances.
But only a short time intervened before she quite
forgot her former state of penury, and by her
excess and extravagance, would soon have
brought her husband to ruin; but he was not a
man to see his hard acquired wealth thus wasted,
and he soon lost all interest in her, and in a
short time she died.

In fact, this retired wealthy merchant had
many wives in succession who died, still leaving
him open to a fresh choice, not that he desired
it, but as it became known that there was again
a chance for another lady to become his wife,
so great was the contention, that he almost
as a defence, was obliged to select one in order
to defend himself against such affectionate assail-
ments.

At length it became the talk and interest of
the part where he resided, respecting the number
of wives he had, and of their deaths; but he held
his peace; now after much importunity from his
friends, many of which had wives who instead of
rendering their husband's lives happy, contributed
by their adverse conduct to the contrary; he told
them the secret, which was that as soon as a wife
became careless, perverse, and dissatisfied, he
allowed her to have her own way, and the result
was that death soon followed.

Then they held long and deliberate councils

amongst the learned and wise men of that part, in order to remedy this state of things, and at length came to the conclusion that a woman's happiness consisted in obedience, and that she was not by nature qualified to oppose that of her husband or father.

They then instituted laws to educate the girls sufficiently so that they should not be at a loss in any society they might marry into, although not to carry it to excess, as if learning was the only thing for which they were born.

There were also other institutions at which all girls were compelled to study, besides what is taught by books ; and whatever position a girl's father was in, either high or low, it mattered not, but she must pass through the full course of the training of these places before she was allowed to marry.

In some of these establishments there was a large number of young children, and after proper instruction each girl had so many children placed under her care, and to present them herself each morning to her superiors, and assist in teaching them ; it was wonderful what interest they generally took in the children submitted to their care.

The next study was a course of instruction in the care and management of infants, and so suc-cessfully was this carried on that illness or death

in infancy or childhood was almost unknown.
And so also was that class of ignorant women
unknown who commence to physic an infant as
soon as it is born—and who stick pins about the
clothing, and say it is displaying its little temper,
when in reality it is in great pain.

There were also large farms where everything
was done according to the very best system.
And the last part of this training was establishments where the preparing and cooking of food
with the strictest regard to cleanliness, economy,
and delicacy, which carried to many a future
household happiness and content. After a girl
had gone through this training she received her
certificate, which was a sufficient guarantee that
she was qualified to manage the ordinary duties
of domestic life.

THE MOUNTAIN OF TROUBLES.

Some people think besides themselves
    That in this world there are no troubles,
And that their load so crushing is,
    And other people's only bubbles.

Ah, what a shame that they should groan,
    Always at work, and have no leisure,
Whilst others always take their ease,
    And think of nothing else but pleasure.

Some possess unbounded wealth,
    And every luxury in season,
Whilst they must live as best they may,
    Is void of right and without reason.

In thinking o'er this varied scene,
　　Sleep stole upon my restless mind ;
I lingered still all this to solve,
　　But yet no remedy could find.

At length I seemed upon a plain,
　　Peopled with countless multitude,
All groaning under burdens sore,
　　So full of grief and platitude.

Each thought his load was heavier far
　　Than any other that could be,
And looked his fellow in the face
　　Expecting help or sympathy.

Then blew a trumpet loud and long,
　　" Give ear," a loud voice did repeat,
" Bring your sore burdens every one,
　　And make of them a common heap."

They flocked thereto, and on a heap
　　Their burdens cast, right glad at heart,
Each uttered imperceptibly,
　　The day has come that we can part.

This heap it grew so wide, so high,
　　And towered toward the firmament,
And shouts arose from all around,
　　So full of glee and merriment.

'Twas then the trumpet blew again,
    Let each another burden take,
Make now your choice for the exchange
    Which shall your future comfort make.

In haste each one a bundle grasped,
    Right glad his own to leave behind ;
But yet when viewed 'twas plain to see,
    It was not suited to his mind.

At last when all had made their choice,
    A shout of discord rent the air,
Weeping and wailing every one
    Groaning in sad and wild despair.

Again the trumpet blew so loud,
    And rent the very atmosphere,
"Return again you sons of men.
    Once more and cast your burdens here."

And each returned in greater haste
    Than he had exercised before,
More loathsome seemed his burden now
    Than that which he had borne before.

The heap again began to rise,
    Once more high up into the air,
But yet it seemed much smaller far
    In height than it had been before.

Then blew the trumpet long and loud,
    This one last choice you now shall make,
And whatsoe'er be its contents,
    No other choice is yours to take.

And all again rushed to the heap,
    But this time exercised more care,
For each was anxious to regain
    The burden they had first brought there.

And so it was that every one
    Their former burden did regain,
And left the scene of discontent,
    Happier far than when they came.

A LAMENT.

Cut down the elms ! for the great, crowded city
   Is wanting green coffins to bury its dead ;
Cut down the elms ! for the suburb extendeth
   Till no view of blue sky shall be seen o'er our head.

Dig up the green turf and groves of choice beeches,
   Fell the grand oaks that have weathered the blast,
Cover the hills all clothed in green verdure,
   Destroy the loved vallies of this land of our birth :

For the great, crowded city comes crushing and pressing
   O'er the beautiful landscape, our glory and pride,
Where the lilies, all clothed in pride and full splendour,
   Are crushed to make room for the great human tide.

Destroy the old hedges, all covered with blossom,
   Spreading the fragrance of beautiful May,
Whilst the lark soaring high, harmoniously explosive,
   Gladdens the heart with his beautiful lay.

Cover the daisies and cowslips so yellow,
   Lilies of the valley and violet banks blue ;
Fill up the stream where the timid trout sporteth,—
   The hand of the spoiler, what more can it do ?

Yes, the sweet-singing songsters that warble so freely,
    And grace with their presence this land of our birth,
Shall soon be extinct, for no place shall be left them
    To cheer with their song and make glad with their
    mirth.

Cover the cornfields, so gracefully bowing
    Their full ears of grain so golden and rare ;
Root up the orchards, with choicest fruits bending,
    That no soil with our own has e'er dared to compare.

For the hand of the spoiler is now fast upon us,
    Brick and mortar will soon reign supreme o'er this
    isle ;
Clouds of smoke shall obscure the blue sky and bright
    sunshine—
    Then farewell to thy produce, oh, Beautiful Isle.

THE DYING CHORISTER.

Are they all there, and singing now,
    Whilst I lie here to die ?
But still our voices yet shall join,
    When we meet in the sky.
My heart—how sad it feels
    To know that I must go,
And leave all those I love so well
    On this earth here below.

I know I ought to feel resigned ;
  This world is passing fast away ;
Yet I may never see again
  The cheering light of day.
My strength seems less each fleeting hour,
  I scarce can draw each breath ;
How strange all seems ! what can this be ?
  Is it—the—hand of Death ?

To-morrow will be Christmas,
  That bright and cheering day,
But, ah ! I seem to feel that then
  I shall be far away.
And you will sing, as I have sung,
  Your voices high will raise,
Where oft I've thought that Heaven's gate
  Would echo with our praise.

Come, mother, kiss my clammy brow,
  My father, take my hand ;
My brothers—yes, I see you now,
  As all around you stand.
Hold up my baby sister,
  That she may look on me,
Before my spirit soars away
  To bright eternity.

STOLEN BY ANGELS.

We had a lovely daughter,
  We called her Little May,
But a brilliant troop of angels came,
  And stole our child away.

And sadly, oh, how sadly
  We missed our little May;
Although she'd been with us three years,
  It seemed but scarce a day.

Her presence was all sunshine,
  We loved her joyous smile!
All day she sung her little songs,
  And seemed our angel child.

Her golden hair was wavy,
  Like glossy, silken thread,
Not kindred to mortality,
  But with heavenly lustre spread.

Her eyes were of the brightest blue,
  More blue than summer sky;
There was gladness in her little face,
  And sunshine in her eye.

Home seems not home without her,
  Yet her memory is so dear;
But—Death—lives but an instant,
  Then all is bright and clear.

But still we see the aged head
  Cling to life through grief and woe ;
And yes, oh yes, the last to come
  Is oft the first to go.

THE EMPTY COT.

The last long breath that baby drew
  Is ever present to my mind,
It softens all my anxious cares,
  And makes me feel calm and resigned.

I look upon the empty cot,
  There lay the toys she claimed her own ;
Her tiny boots and pinafore
  To me are priceless, now she's gone.

Whilst she was here my life was bright,
  A mother's joy and care was mine,
But now she's gone, all is dark and drear,
  Like clouds that veil the clear blue sky.

O yes, my babe, my only child,
  A gift from heaven, so choice, so rare ;
God grant when I shall also go,
  In heaven that I may claim thee there.

But there came bright angels from far away,
And took my baby to endless day.
Gone, my precious baby, gone far away,
To dwell with brightest angels.

I COULD NOT SAY FAREWELL.

I could not say Farewell that day,
  I could not say Farewell,
For my heart was sad and heavy,
  More than language scarce could tell.

I knew long years must pass away
  Ere I came back again,
But the thought that pressed upon me was
  Should I find you still the same ?

I knew the mighty ocean
  Would bear me to a shore
Where dreams are often realized
  Of gold made o'er and o'er.

But in leaving you, and all I loved,
    Was more than words could tell ;
It was *that*, my love, prevented me,
    I could not say Farewell.

But now those years have passed away,
    And I am back again,
My fondest hopes are realized,
    For you are still the same.

The happy days are come at last,
    As we may proudly tell,
Therefore, my love, there is no need
    For us to say " Farewell."

CONRAD'S COURAGE.

A noble ship was the Alpine Wave,
    As it proudly sailed away,
Its bleached white sails all fully set,
    As it dashed through the foam and spray.

And onward it sped on its distant way,
    With light hearts, stout and strong,
For a gallant crew had the Alpine Wave,
    As it proudly swept along.

The sun shone forth in its summer power,
  And all was joy and glee,
For a statelier ship, with cargo rich,
  Ne'er sped o'er the mighty sea.

But a tempest rose with fearful might,
  And thunder rolled so loud,
And lightnings glittered incessantly,
  Severing the angry clouds.

And on this ship was a fair, fair child,
  A father's only son,
Returning again to distant lands,
  Where honest wealth had been fairly won.

The father took his loving boy,
  And bound him to the mast,
Thinking his safety to secure,
  Till that raging storm was past.

The reddening light of morning
  The turbid sea breaks o'er,
And dims the lighted headlands
  Along the stretching shore.

And many anxious hearts on shore
  Had quailed through this fearful night,
And in haste sped forth to the water's brink
  At the dawn of morning's light.

And many a powerful glass was there,
   That swept o'er the mighty main,
And silence ruled anxiety,
   Until more trusty daylight came.

It was then that the ship lay full in view,
   And the waters flowed its deck,
No hopes appeared of human life,
   For the ship lay a perfect wreck.

The sea-gulls hover round the shore,
   With wild and timid cry,
Whilst the billows mock their plaintive notes
   To mute obscurity.

But many a powerful telescope
   On this sight was brought to bear,
And tears were on the cheeks of those
   That viewed from the sandy shore.

Plainly the fair child could be seen
   Lashed to the rising mast,
Its golden hair so flowingly
   A sport to the mighty blast.

But sad it was that willing hands,
   As it were, quite powerlessly
Seemed paralyzed in wild despair
   At this maddened raging sea.

Then came forth brave young Conrad,
His step, though light, was firm,
His eye glanced o'er the dashing waves
And the boiling froth and foam.

All anxious eyes were turned on him,
As some garments he cast aside,
An instant more—he was firmly clasped
In the arms of his three days' bride.

He bid her a loving, fond adieu,
She blessed him as he went ;
A moment more, he had left the shore
To battle the elements.

The sea-gulls hover o'er his head
With wild and timid cry,
As if in lamentation
That no other help was nigh.

He is gone ! he is lost ! sad voices cry,
He is choked in the mighty sea !
God grant that his soul for this brave act
May inhabit eternity.

Each anxious moment, each tearful eye,
With long abated breath—
Then shouts rose simultaneously,
His feet tread the fearful wreck.

Cautious and slow his steady eye,
    For sad was the scene he views,
Red-streaked clouds high above his head,
    O'er his feet the rough water flows.

But a gentle shriek, a fainter moan,
    Attracts his vacant ear,
His eyes are raised to the topmost mast,
    For the child is fettered there.

Gently he unbinds the cords,
    The father's loving hand
Most tenderly had bound his child,
    So far from the distant land.

That boy's bright eyes they looked on him
    With wild and timid stare,
As if afraid of every hand
    But the one that had bound him there.

And now again to the mighty waves
    Bravely he bears his charge;
His arm is strong, his courage stout
    To encounter the foam and surge.

He laboured on, as if to eclipse
    The wild and dashing spray,
But mightier blasts successively
    Soon swept him far away.

At every.bound the waters flash
　As lightnings from on high,
Like sea birds sweeping in the deep,
　To mount again on high.

A thousand breaths suspended
　Upon the distant shore,
And feared the sight they looked upon
　Could reach the sands no more.

And many a maid and matron
　Drew long, long breaths and sighed,
For all loved brave young Conrad,
　And blessed his three days' bride.

But still again he nears the shore,
　Tossed by the waves so wild ;
He treads the sands, he is safe once more,
　He has saved the fair, fair child !